Hearts Blazing

By Tina Velazquez

PublishAmerica
Baltimore

© 2008 by Tina Velazquez.
All rights reserved. No part of this book may be reproduced, stored in a retrieval system or transmitted in any form or by any means without the prior written permission of the publishers, except by a reviewer who may quote brief passages in a review to be printed in a newspaper, magazine or journal.

First printing

All characters in this book are fictitious, and any resemblance to real persons, living or dead, is coincidental.

PublishAmerica has allowed this work to remain exactly as the author intended, verbatim, without editorial input.

ISBN: 1-60610-218-4 (softcover)
ISBN: 978-1-4489-0826-4 (hardcover)
PUBLISHED BY PUBLISHAMERICA, LLLP
www.publishamerica.com
Baltimore

Printed in the United States of America

This book is dedicated to my husband, Raul. Without his encouragement and confidence in me, I would not have been able to write this. He was my inspiration. He was the one that brought true love into my life and showed me that nothing is impossible. Without him, I would not know that there is such a thing called fate. I thank God everyday for bringing him into my life.

Chapter 1

It was supposed to be the happiest day of a woman's life. The church blossomed with beautiful, colorful flowers. The bridesmaids lingered in their baby blue dresses; the groomsmen in their black tuxes. Friends and relatives all so excited for the young couple filled the church. The groom stood in anticipation at the altar for his beautiful bride. I could picture all this clearly as I waited in the back room with my maid of honor and best friend, Jan. My mind raced, knowing that soon I would walk down the aisle. Thinking that, in a few minutes, I would lay eyes upon my eager, soon-to-be husband. Wondering how I was going to be able to go through with this after what happened last night.

It just happened. It wasn't planned. What is planned is this wedding. Planned down to the very last little detail. I know everyone is out there waiting for me to make my entrance into my new life. I know I have to go through with this. I can't disappoint the man who had come to love me so much over the months that he was willing to go to any length for me. He adored and worshiped me. I just had to do this…didn't I?

The image of last night burned in my mind. The arms of another man. The passion that was never there with Zack. I had to somehow forget it. But how? How could I forget those deep feelings, the feelings of real love that I only have for Jonathan?

Just go, I told myself, and do what you have made a commitment to do…

5

1 Year Ago

Another long day in the cleaning business. It's like the days just blend into each other, with nothing to look forward to at the end of the day. Nothing, that is, except this old house that I've come to love. The house that needs so much repair and updating that it will cost a fortune when I finally get around to it.

Of all the rooms in the house, the kitchen is the worst. I have hated that kitchen since the day I moved in. That was twenty-six years ago, but everything takes money. Money I don't have.

Thinking back on my day, it seemed to be quite unusual. My first client, Millie, talked and talked the whole time I cleaned her house. She followed me from room to room throughout the entire house.

"I don't understand why you don't date. You're still young! It's such a waste that you're turning your back on all men just because of a few sour apples!"

"Really Millie, I just don't have the time. Sundays are my only days off and sometimes not even then. If I do have the day off, I either have so much catching up to do around the house or I'm too tired. Besides, who would go out with a workaholic? A workaholic with an old house and no money?"

"You underestimate men. They're not all bad. I think I'll fix you up with my nephew. He'd be good for you. At least just go out with him."

"Oh no you don't! I don't do dates, let alone blind dates."

"We'll see," was all she said as she paid me for my time, along with a five-dollar tip.

"See you next week Millie, and remember, no funny stuff." At that I got into my car and drove off to the next job.

Mary was a sweet little old lady. Two years ago, she lost her husband, Joe, to cancer. But even now, he was all she talked about.

HEARTS BLAZING

She was eighty-seven years old and she and Joe had been together since they were eighteen. *Love at first sight* is how Mary describes it. She knew from the moment she met him that he was the one for her, and he felt the same. Now that she's all alone, Mary is often lonely. She doesn't even need me weekly, but has me come anyway, just for the company.

"Tara, oh I'm so glad to see you! I just made some tea. Do you want some?"

"Now you know I'm here to clean... not drink tea," I laughed. She asked me this same question every week and every week she knew my answer.

"How you doing today Mary?"

"Oh I'm ok, just a little tired."

As I cleaned, I thought about what Millie said. She couldn't be serious about setting me up with her nephew. What was she thinking? Although, I had to admit it would be nice to have someone to come home to at night. And even to go out with once in awhile.

Mary came into the kitchen and asked me what I'd been up to lately. Of course, my answer was the same as always.

"Nothing... just working.

"Work! Is that all you ever do?"

"Well, yeah, it seems to be my life."

"Well, you need to go out and have some fun! You know... I have a grandson."

"Oh not you too!" I exclaimed.

"Whatever do you mean? All I said was I have a grandson."

"Yeah... and he'd be perfect for me, right?"

"Well now that you put it that way, he might be. Just think! Maybe you can be my granddaughter-in-law."

"Oh please! I don't even date and you've already got me married?"

"Well, l stranger things have happened!"

7

TINA VELAZQUEZ

"Not to me, but thanks for thinking of me," I sighed.

"No problem my dear. Keep him in mind if you ever change your mind."

"I will sweetie. I just finished my cleaning, so you be good and I'll see you next week." Off I went again to my next house. As I pulled up in front of Martha's house I noticed a man on her porch. It looked like he was fixing her door. As I approached the porch, arms loaded with cleaning supplies, the man looked up.

"You must be Tara? Martha told me you'd be coming through this door soon."

"Yeah, I clean for her every week just to give her a helping hand."

"That's nice! It must be a very rewarding job."

"Yeah it is. I like being able to help people out, especially the elderly. Of course, it also pays the bills! But I think enjoying your work is what really counts."

"I agree. It can be hard to find a job like that. Well here, let me get the door for you. It's fallen half off its hinges so I'm hanging it back up for her."

"Thanks," I replied. As he opened the door, I noticed he had the bluest eyes I had ever seen. They were almost transparent.

"Thanks again," I said.

"No problem, anytime."

"Oh by the way, my name's Zack. Do you have a business card or phone number I could have? I deal with a lot of people in my line of work. I might be able to throw some cleaning jobs your way."

"Thanks," I said. I'll go get you one before I leave. They're in my car."

"Ok. I'll be here a few hours still, so I'm sure you'll be leaving before me. Martha says you get here, get down to business and are gone before you could say boo!"

"I guess I'm pretty quick! I've been doing this forever."

"I know what you mean. I've been in the door and window

8

HEARTS BLAZING

business since I was out of high school. It pays the bills."

Martha must have overheard us talking, because a second later she appeared at the door. "Tara, you're here! I thought I heard you talking! I see you met Zack."

"Yeah, we were just getting to know each other. But now I have to get to work. I'll bring you some business cards when I'm done, Zack."

And to work I got! I finished the bathroom first, then the kitchen, then went in the bedroom to dust. Sitting on the dresser were the same photos I have seen every week while cleaning Martha's house. They were photos of Martha and her husband: at their wedding, at a party, at a friend's house. Frank died three years ago. Martha had been the sparkle in his eye. He adored her and she him. She hadn't remarried. She once told me, "There could be no one that could take the place of my Frank. We were so in love. We knew each other like an open book. We knew what the other was going to say before we said it and what we were going to do before we did it. I couldn't ever be so close to someone like that again. I wouldn't want to. We'll meet again someday and until then... he's here with me. He's in my heart and my soul and he always will be. I don't need anyone to fill my days and nights. I have my memories, my photos and my love and one day we'll be together again for all eternity. I could never find another love like ours." I hope that one day I can find a love like that.

When I went back into the front room, Martha was talking to Zack. "Doors are done," he said.

"Guess I beat you today, Tara! Now how about those business cards before I leave," he asked.

"Sure, no problem. Let me run and get some cards from my car."

I picked up a handful of business cards and went back to the house. Stepping back into the front room, I noticed Martha and Zack both smiling at me. "What's wrong," I asked.

"Oh nothing's wrong! I was just telling Zack what a hard worker

9

TINA VELAZQUEZ

you are and that you've been with me for years."

"Oh, ok. Well here's my card, Zack. I gave you a few extras."

"Here is mine too." He handed me the card and I noticed that the address was just in the next town. "Well it was really nice meeting you Tara. Hope I see you again sometime. Maybe we could each throw some business each other's way."

'It was nice meeting you too Zach. I think that would be great if we could drum up some business for each other."

"Drive safe and take care of yourself," Zack said. Martha and I watched him as he walked to his truck.

"Such a nice man," she said. He's single you know. Never been married. Said he never found the right girl."

"Oh really? Yeah he's not bad," I said. I tried to sound nonchalant, but all I could think about were his eyes. Back in the house, I finished my visit to Martha's by dusting and vacuuming the front room. Time to be on my way again.

I had about a half hour before my next appointment, so I decided to get gas and stop at the store for some bread and peanut butter. Walking into the store, I noticed an ad for someone selling wolf hybrid puppies. I've always loved wolves and it would be a dream come true to own one. These wolf hybrids are probably the closest I could ever get. I wrote the phone number down, thinking I just might call when I get home.

Chapter 2

Jill wasn't feeling well when I got to her house. I made her a cup of tea before starting to clean. She was my last appointment for the day, so I took my time.

Driving home later on, my mind seemed to be in a whirl. I couldn't stop thinking about my life, about my jobs, about the wolf puppy add and especially about the man with the blue eyes.

I walked into the house and carried my bags into the kitchen. As I walked past the phone, I noticed my answering machine light flashing. Of course, this wasn't unusual; with all the clients I had someone was always calling for something. I hit the button on the machine and the messages began to play. One call was from Helen. She wanted to make sure I'd be at her house tomorrow. I was always there on the same day, at the same time every week and yet she always called the day before to make sure I was coming. She was funny.

The next call was from June. She wanted to know if I had any openings because she had a friend that needed my services. The last call was from Zack. He wanted to tell me that he really enjoyed meeting and talking to me and wanted to know if we could get together on Sunday. He said to call him anytime when I got home he'd be there and be looking forward to my call.

As I walked away from the phone, I wondered whether I should call him back or just forget about him. I decided to make my decision over a cup of tea. As I was drinking my tea, the phone rang. It was Zack.

11

"Hey your home!" he began.

"Oh hi! I just got in about twenty minutes ago and got your message. I was going to call you after I had my tea."

"So you're a teetotaler," he laughed.

"Yeah that's about as strong as it gets," I said.

"Well listen, I wanted to know if we could get together and hang out on Sunday. Whatever you want would be fine with me. I know that's your only day off."

"That it is! You know, I usually like to just stay home since I'm away from home so much with work," I said.

"I understand. How about if I just come over and to watch a movie or something? I'll bring a pizza for dinner."

"Yeah, I guess that would be all right," I said.

"Ok then, I'll be over about two o'clock ok"?

"Sure, see you then," I said as I hung up the phone. Oh no, what did I just do? How could I have agreed to this? Oh well. I agreed to it, so who knows; maybe it'll be nice.

My mind wandered from Zack to the ad for the wolf puppies and decided to call for more information. I dug through my pocket for the phone number. A lady answered my call. "Hi I was calling about the wolf hybrid pups you have for sale?"

"Yes, well I have five of them. They're wolf and husky mix. Eight weeks old and they're adorable!"

"How much would they be? And where do you live? I asked.

She replied that she lived only about five miles from me and that the price was one hundred fifty dollars. "Can I come and see them?" I asked

"Sure, when would you like to?"

"Just let me know a good day and time for you."

"Anytime is ok for me. I'm home all day," she said.

"How about tomorrow at around two o'clock? I have an early day tomorrow." I knew I only had two houses tomorrow so I'd be able to go then.

HEARTS BLAZING

"That sounds great," she said.

She gave me her address and we said our goodbyes. I went in the kitchen and began to wash the dishes, vowing one day that I'd get this kitchen remodeled. No matter how hard I'll have to work. Suddenly I remembered that June called wanting to know if I had any other openings, so I called her back. "Hi June. It's Tara returning your call."

"Hi Tara. I was calling about a friend of mine, Alice. Things around the house are getting too hard for her to take care of herself. I just had to tell her about you. She wants you to give her a call if you have any free time."

"Sure, I can do that. What's her phone number?"

After she gave me Alice's phone number, I told June that I'd give Alice a call and that I would see her tomorrow as usual.

I called the number and got an answer right away.

"Hello?"

"Hi, my name is Tara. June gave me your number. She said you were looking for someone to clean for you once a week."

"Oh yes my dear, June told me you'd call. It's just getting so hard for me to vacuum lately. I'm not as young as I use to be," she laughed. "The dusting's not so bad, but washing the floors has gotten hard too. June says you've been with her for two years and she highly recommends you."

"Oh, thank you. Yes, I've been with June for quite awhile. She's such a sweet lady. I'd be able to come to clean for you on Fridays if that's ok?"

"That would be fine. I'm always home."

We made arrangements for me to start this Friday, the day after tomorrow. It was getting late and I was exhausted! So I went and took a shower, had another cup of tea and feel fast asleep.

Chapter 3

The next morning I woke early as usual. I was so excited that the workday would be short and then I could go see the wolf puppies! I arrived at Helen's house at ten o'clock on the dot. "Hi Helen how are you?"

"Oh I'm fine honey. You know me, just watching my morning news show."

"I got your call yesterday Miss Helen. Just like I do *every* week!"

"Oh I know! I'm such a pain. I just have no one to talk to and so I just call.'

"I'm only kidding Helen! It's fine that you call. I just wish I would have been home to talk to you."

"That's ok Tara. I at least got to hear your voice on the answering machine... and the best part is that you're here now!"

I started to tell Helen about Zack, who I had met just yesterday, and about how his planned visit on Sunday.

"That's wonderful! You need a nice man like that in your life. You're so young and you have so much to offer."

"I guess I don't feel so young some days."

"We all get like that honey. Wait until you're my age."

"Come on Helen, you're still a spring chicken and you know it!" I laughed. I went on to tell her how I was going to look at some wolf puppies. I told her how I have been amazed by and loved wolves for years. That I had statues and pictures all over my house. And that I

HEARTS BLAZING

even sponsored some at a wolf foundation! Their beauty was remarkable. To actually own one even if it was only half wolf, would be a dream come true. I got done with Helen's house said my goodbye's. Then I got in the car to drive to June's. When I arrived, June was sitting on the front porch. She seemed to be enjoying the nice weather, unseasonably high in the seventies.

"Hey there," I said as I got out of the car.

"Hi! How are things going?" June replied.

"Not too bad. I got a hold of your friend Alice, I'm going to help her out tomorrow."

"Oh I'm glad! She really needs your help. Things are getting hard for her lately."

"You don't have to worry about her any more. I'll take care of her."

"I knew you would. That's why I just had to call you! You know, I wish I had someone to fix my window in the back. It won't open anymore and you know I like my fresh air. Not that air conditioning!"

"Well, you're in luck! I met someone yesterday at a client's house and that just happens to be what he does for a living. I have his phone number in my car. I'll get it for you."

As I walked back to the car, I turned and told June, "In fact he's coming over Sunday with pizza to watch a movie."

June clasped her hand in front of her chest and exclaimed, "Oh please don't give me a heart attack! You're actually going to date again? I thought you swore off men for life!" she smiled.

"Ok. Ok. So I did. But I'm a woman. I have a right to change my mind."

I went to the car and got Zack's number. Then brought it back to the porch and gave it to her.

"Should I call him now?" she asked.

"Go ahead, he might answer. If not, leave a message."

15

TINA VELAZQUEZ

June and I walked into the house. As I was getting water in the kitchen, she called Zack. "Hi, my name's June, Tara gave me your number. She said you might be able to fix my kitchen window that won't open anymore." She paused. "Yes, I understand. Oh, well she's here now. Ok, that would be fine, as long as I'm not taking you away from anything important! Well here's my address."

I was in the bathroom cleaning when June came in. "Well you must have left some impression on this man! I told him what was wrong and he said he was leaving his house to go finish a job, but he could stop by tomorrow. Then I told him you were here and he just about jumped through the phone saying he could be here in twenty minutes to look at it!"

"Well that just means he wanted a break from the other job."

"Oh please. I wasn't born yesterday! You must have really left a lasting impression."

"Why, what ever do you mean Miss June," I said. We both laughed. Exactly twenty minutes later the doorbell rang. I was finishing up in the kitchen when Zack walked in.

"Hey good to see you again," he said.

"You too! Long time no see," I laughed. Here's the window June said won't budge."

"Well let's have a look at what could be wrong."

I finished cleaning out the microwave as he was looking at the window, but I couldn't help to feel him staring at me. When I looked up he was smiling. "You look so cute when you're cleaning," he said.

"Oh get out of here. You must need glasses."

"Nope, perfect twenty-twenty vision here."

As he spoke, June walked into the kitchen. "Well what seems to be wrong with the window?"

"Nothing big. Just off the track some and could use a little oil." Zack said he could have it fixed in a jiffy.

16

We both got done with our jobs at about the same time. I told June I'd see her next week. He told her if she had any more problems to call.

As I got back to the car and was getting ready to put my cleaning supplies in the trunk, Zack came running up. "Whoa, let me get that for you." As he put everything in my trunk, he asked where I was off to next.

"If I told you I'm sure you wouldn't believe me," I said.

"Try me," he laughed.

I told him about the wolf pups I was going to look at.

"You're kidding?"

"I told you that you wouldn't believe me!"

"Let me go with you. Just for the ride, so you don't have to go alone."

"Don't you have more work today?" I asked.

"It could wait. I'd rather go with you."

He seemed very sincere, so how could I say no? "Get in. We'll come back for your truck," I said. It took about a half hour to get to the address the lady gave me on the phone. When we got there, I rang the bell. A pretty, dark haired lady answered the door. I told her I had called the night before about the wolf pups.

"Oh yes, I remember. Come on in, they have their own bedroom with their mom."

Zack rolled his eyes at this, but I thought it was great that these wolf pups were spoiled! I loved to see people take extra special care of God's little creatures.

When we got to the room, all the pups started yipping! They were in this big wooden homemade box with all kinds of pillows and quilts. They almost looked as if they were homemade too! "Oh they are so cute."

Again, I noticed Zack roll his eyes, which was a little odd to me. He didn't even seem to like the pups at all. I only noticed this for a moment, though; because the pups made me so happy to be with them that it didn't matter.

I asked the lady all kinds of questions and finally decided to take two of them, so they wouldn't be lonely. I looked at all of the adorable pups and decided on two girls. I remembered to bring a big blanket with me, just in case, and it's a good thing I did because I knew right away I'd be taking at least one home.

When we got back to town, I dropped Zack off at his truck and told him I'd see him Sunday. Then I was on my way home with my new family!

Taking the box with the pups out of the back seat, I walked up to the house. They were yipping and trying to crawl out of the box as I walked up the walkway. I couldn't stop laughing at how cute they were! "What am I going to name you little ones? You are so adorable."

When I got in the house, I sat on the floor with them. I pulled their blanket out of the box and bunched it up on the floor. "I guess I'll let you two sleep in my room tonight. I have to keep an eye on you after all." I gave each a kiss on the top of their head and it was time for bed.

Chapter 4

The pups slept really well that night. I was worried they'd miss their mother, but I didn't hear a peep out of them at all. I only had to go to my new client, Alice, today so I had all morning with the little ones. The phone rang at around ten thirty.

"Hi! How are your babies doing?" Zack asked.

"Hey, really good. They slept through the night. They're sleeping now too. I fed them and played with them this morning and I guess I wore them out!"

"Do you have to work today?"

"Yeah, only one appointment though at noon."

"How about if I come over around four? I'll bring some chicken."

"You don't have to do that."

"I know I don't have to. I want to, if you'll let me that is. Today's only Friday and Sunday just seems so far away to be able to see you again. Please say yes?"

"Oh alright then. Four o'clock is ok. I'll be home."

The new lady, Alice, was really nice. She had a three-bedroom house and lived there alone. Her husband passed away some twenty years ago. She had two children, but they both lived out of state so she really didn't have anyone except her friend June. As soon as I got started, Alice began telling me about all the other things she needed done around the house. She said she wished she knew a handyman.

TINA VELAZQUEZ

"You and me both," I told her. "My kitchen is from the 1920's and I'd really like to update it, but everything cost so much money! And then I'd have to try to find the right person to do it too."

"Do you have any spare time during the week, Tara? I know June said your really busy, but it would be nice if I could hire you a few days a week just to sit and talk with me. It gets so lonely here."

"Well Mondays, Tuesdays and Saturdays for a few hours in the early afternoon would be ok. Does that sound good?"

"Oh that would be perfect. Maybe you could take me to the store sometimes too?

"Sure that'd be no trouble."

"Ok, so now that we have that settled, you better let me start cleaning! I have two new wolf puppies at home and I don't want to leave them for long."

"Oh my goodness! Would you bring them with you next time? I love wolves. They're so beautiful."

"Oh you really wouldn't mind?"

"Of course not! I'd be thrilled. This house has been quiet for way too long."

"Then yes, when I come back on Monday I'll have them with me. You could be their Grandma."

When I got back home, the pups were rolling around playing with each other in their pen. They looked up at me and immediately started yipping. They were both trying to jump out at me so I had to take them out and hold them. They were both trying to climb all over me and kiss my face. I was laughing so hard I fell back on the floor as they climbed all over me. "I suppose you're hungry? Starving right? Well let me go get you your food." I looked at the clock and saw that it was already three o'clock. One hour and Zack would be here. Better get these pups fed. And they still needed names too! I noticed that one was always hiding behind the other, so I decided to name her Shadow while her sister I named Mya.

20

HEARTS BLAZING

I took a quick shower while they ate and by the time I dressed the doorbell was ringing. "Hey, your ten minutes early!"

"I could wait out here or come back?"

"Don't be silly. Come on in," I said, still brushing my hair.

"Well, look at these little ones crawling all over their pen with food all over the place," he commented, looking not too pleased.

"Yeah I know. I just fed them. I still need to change their paper."

Zack watched as I cleaned up the pups. Then I went and grabbed plates to bring into the front room for the chicken he had brought. "We'll wind down and TV as we eat if you don't mind."

"No, whatever you want is fine with me."

We ate and watched TV. Then I gave him a tour of the house as the pups curled up together, fast asleep. Zack was forty-six years old; never married lived in the next town, had no children, no pets and owned his own house. Sounded like a good catch.

The phone rang and I picked it up. It was my friend Jan. "Hey what's going on?" she asked.

"Nothing, I was just sitting here with Zack watching TV You'll never guess what I got yesterday! Two wolf hybrid puppies. They are so cute. They're sleeping now all curled up together."

"Wait a minute," Jan said. "Your watching TV with who? Who's this? You never told me about anyone named Zack."

"I know. I'll tell you later."

"No tell me now!" she moaned.

I knew Zack was listening, so I just smiled at him and told her how I met him. Then I said, "Ok Jan, be nice and say hi to Zack." I handed him the phone and told him to say hi to Jan. She's been my friend forever. They said hi to each other and he handed me the phone back.

"He sounds nice! I better let you go. Be good and call me tomorrow," she said.

"Yeah I will. Take care."

21

Jan and I had been friends since high school. She was currently in a troubled marriage, worked at a church, and was just lonely for the love of the husband she once knew. When we finished high school and Jan got married everything was fine, but as the years went by her husband started drinking heavily. Now I'd even classify him an alcoholic. The only time Jan ever felt happy was when she got out of the house and came to visit me. Anything to get away from his verbal abuse. I had to remember to call her tomorrow and tell her to come see the pups. That'd cheer her up.

We finished watching the movie and I told Zack, "I don't want to be rude, but I really needed to feed the pups. It's been a long day." That was the truth! I was really tired, so we agreed he'd come over on Sunday with pizza as planned. I walked him to the door.

"I'm really glad you let me unexpectedly come over today. I really wanted to spend some time with you. I enjoyed every minute."

"Thanks, me too," replied. I watched him walk to his truck and when he got there, he turned and waved. Then he beeped as he drove away.

As for me, it was time to feed my adorable pups.

Chapter 5

The pups slept really well again that night. The next morning I got up and fed them. Then I brought them out in the yard to try to start training them. I figured that was the thing to do. After all, they are part of the dog family.

After training, we came in the house and played for about an hour with some little toys. I must have tired them out because they both fell fast asleep! I was excited to have today and tomorrow off work. It was very unusual for me to have two days off in a row! I decided to call Jan and see if she wanted to come see the pups later on.

She answered on the second ring. "Hello?"

"Hey Jan it's me."

"Oh am I glad to hear from you! This man is driving me crazy. I don't know how much longer I can go on with this life. He got so drunk last night he passed out on the floor."

"Oh poor you! I don't know how you can stand it. What are you doing today?"

"Nothing much. I have to go to the store, but that's about it."

"Why don't you come by and see Mya and Shadow?"

"Oh what cute names! I can't wait to see them. You mean your not working today?"

"No. I'm off today and tomorrow," I said.

"I think I might faint! I can't believe you actually took a day off," Jan said.

TINA VELAZQUEZ

"Well I did, but I got another job from one of my clients. I'll tell you about it when you get here."

"Yeah, and you better tell me all about this Zack too."

"Oh yeah... him too."

"Ok I should be there around five o'clock."

"Ok, see you then." I put the phone down and was just about to go put a load of clothes in the washer when the phone rang.

"Hello? Hey there! What are you doing," I asked Zack.

"Nothing. I just finished a job and decided to call you. What are you doing?"

"I just fed the little guys and was about to wash some clothes."

"Oh, sounds fun. You wouldn't want some company would you? I'd love to come see you again."

"Well I think you'll have to wait until tomorrow. I have to go shopping and Jan's coming over to see the pups at five. She'll probably stay until at least seven."

"Ok, seven it is then. Want me to bring some food? What do you want? Mexican, Italian or Chinese?" he asked.

"No, you don't have to bring me food all the time. How about if I make us spaghetti?"

"Yeah, that sounds great! I'll see you then. Oh and Tara?"

"Yeah?"

"I miss you LOTS!"

"Oh you're just being silly. I'll see you at seven." I hung up the phone thinking it was nice to have someone thinking about me. It had been a long time since I really cared for anyone or had anyone care for me. It seemed like most men I met were never satisfied with what they had and were always looking for something better. I hoped Zack wasn't like that. I didn't think he was, or else why would he always be calling me and wanting to come over? After all, we'd only known each other a few days. I called Alice before I went to the store to see if she needed anything that I could bring with me on Monday.

"Oh yes! Bring me some tea, sugar, lettuce and a chocolate candy bar. I love my sweets. You'll find that out after you've been here for a few days. I have to have my chocolate," she laughed.

I laughed as I hung up the phone and left for the store.

When I got back home, the pups were just waking up. "Hi Mya... hi Shadow. Come on you guys, let's go outside then I'll feed you both again." I knew that was the way to train dogs and I figured that this was really no different. They are just the cutest things. I'm glad Alice said I could bring them with me on Monday, because I don't think I could bear to leave them.

When we went outside, they seemed to be quick learners! They did just what they were supposed to do. We came back in the house after that and they ate like two little starving wolves, making cute little sounds as they gobbled the food. I decided to make the spaghetti since Jan would be over in a few hours. That way when Zack got here later, all I'd have to do is reheat it.

"Come on Mya... come on Shadow... let's go out again now that you're done eating." They went back out right away again and I played ball with them for a while in the yard. I could hear the doorbell ring so we went back inside and I answered the door. It was Jan.

"Hi! My goodness! These are some wolves!" she exclaimed as she walked in.

I hadn't put them back in their little pen yet and they were scampering around on the floor. 'Yeah what'd you think?"

"Oh they are so cute! I want one."

"Well the lady's got a few left!"

"Oh Tara, you are so lucky. Where did you ever find them?"

I told her how I saw the ad in the store and how I knew I had to take at least one home with me.

"Well you've got your hands full now, but I'd rather have this than what I have at home." She went on to tell me how bad her husband was drinking lately and how mentally abusive he had been. She started crying and I told her she really had to do what she knew she had to do.

That was my motto. "You gotta do what you gotta do." She knew this and started laughing.

"Yeah, but I'm not as strong as you are Tara."

"You underestimate yourself. Do you think it was easy for me when I got my divorce? Of course not, but it was better than staying in the marriage I was in. If you could even call it a marriage. The last years we were together we basically lived separate lives. To even look at him made me ill."

"Don't worry Tara. I'll be ok. Tell me all about Zack!"

I told her how we met and that he'd been calling and visiting me ever since. "In fact, he's coming for spaghetti later."

"Oh wow! Why can't I meet a nice guy like that?"

We sat and drank some wine coolers and just talked about our jobs and our lives. I told her about Alice and how I was going to be going over there three days a week.

"See, there you go taking another job. Maybe this Zack will be able to slow you down some," she said.

"Oh stop. What else do I have to do anyway?"

"Well now you have these adorable little guys to take care of. That should keep you busy."

"Yeah, aren't they cute?" I hadn't put them back in their little play area yet, so they were still rolling around on the floor in a blanket together. I walked in the kitchen to get us another wine cooler out of the refrigerator. I yelled out to Jan, "Oh I hate this kitchen!"

She started laughing saying, "You've hated that kitchen ever since I met you. Maybe Zack could fix it for you."

"First off, he doesn't do that kind of work and even if he did I wouldn't expect him to."

"Well, one day you'll get it done. I know you too well. When you

HEARTS BLAZING

set your mind to something, you make it happen."

We sat there watching the pups and drinking our wine coolers. A little while later Jan said she had to get going.

"I can't imagine what I'll be going home to now. Probably a passed out husband."

"Well, call me if you need me... and don't be so hard on yourself. You're a good person... he's the one doing wrong."

She lived right around the block, so I watched her until she turned the corner. I wish she realized she deserved so much better.

Zack pulled up as I started to walk back to the house, so I waited for him. He walked up smiling with his hands behind his back. When he got to the porch, he pulled his hands out from behind his back and displayed a huge bouquet of flowers. "Beautiful flowers for my beautiful lady... inside and out."

"Oh Zack, they are beautiful!" I kissed his cheek.

"Whoa, I'll bring you a whole yard full of flowers for another kiss."

"Oh, you get out of here. Come on, I'll heat up dinner. You're probably starving if you haven't eaten yet."

"No I'm ok. Here let me get that for you." He held the door open and we walked into the house. The pups were fast asleep on the floor in the blanket. They had worn themselves out. "So how was your visit with Jan"?

"It was very nice. She loved the pups. She said she'd like to have one herself."

"Well the lady has some left... why doesn't she go get one?"

"With the problems she has right now with her husband, I think she has her hands full."

We ate our spaghetti and watched TV. Before I knew it, time had flown by and it was ten o'clock. When I told Zack it was getting late, he asked if I had a radio. I told him I had one, but it wasn't out here, it was in the bedroom.

27

"Well if you put it on. Can we hear it in here?" he asked.

"Yeah I suppose we can. Why?"

He told me the number for a slow jazz station. I went to the bedroom and turned the radio up. When a song came on, he got up off the couch and took me in his arms saying, "You don't know how long I've wanted to do this or how good it feels to hold you. I haven't cared for a woman in a long time Tara."

The song ended and another one came on. We danced through that song too as he held me in his arms and started kissing my neck. That's when it happened. I could feel it coming. I was so nervous as he held me in his arms and looked down at me. "I'm so glad I was at Martha's house that day or I would have never met you," he whispered. He held me close as his lips met mine. "Oh Tara, let me make you happy."

His kiss became more urgent, more demanding of my lips. He had a strength that I wasn't sure he even knew he had. Surprisingly though, I really didn't feel much from his kiss. There was no butterfly effect. I realized that this was going too fast for me, so I pulled away.

"Zack, I like you a lot, but I'm not really ready for this. You're going a little too fast for me. I'm not ready for anything serious yet, so can we just take it slow?"

"Of course Tara. I'm sorry, I didn't mean to scare you."

"You didn't scare me. It's just that I was in a bad relationship recently and I'm not ready to rush into anything I might regret later. Do you understand?"

"I understand. I'll take it as slow as you want because I believe you're worth waiting for no matter how long it takes."

"Thanks" I said as I pulled out of his arms.

As that was said the pups were starting to stir.

"Looks like someone's hungry again. Want me to help you," he asked?

"Yeah, but first let's take them out. I'm starting to train them.

HEARTS BLAZING

We took them out then brought them in to feed them. We sat there watching them and laughing as they ate. You would have thought they had never been fed before. They made the cutest little growling noises as they ate.

"Well, I guess it's getting late and you need some sleep. I'll be back tomorrow with dinner. Remember, you already agreed to me bringing Sunday's dinner."

"Yeah I remember, but it seems like you been bringing food over every day!"

He gave me another kiss and said, "Dream of me sweetheart. I know I'll dream of you."

I watched him as he walked to his truck and got in. He beeped as he drove away.

After he left, I went back in the house to settle the pups in for the night and get ready for bed. It had been a long day.

Chapter 6

The next day, on Sunday, I woke up and started my routine of taking the pups outside, then feeding them, then taking them outside again. I had a lazy morning just drinking coffee and watching Mya and Shadow play. I knew they weren't full-blooded wolves, but they sure looked like it to me. I was convinced they were more wolf than husky.

The doorbell rang around two o'clock. I went to answer it and there he was with his hands full again. "Zack, it looks like you brought enough for an army! This is more than just pizza," I laughed.

"No, it's just for us and for you for tomorrow when you get home from work. I don't want you to have to worry about food or cooking when you get home from working all day. Besides I'll be here to help you eat it."

"You spoil me Zack. I'm going to forget how to cook."

"I'm sure you'll never forget how to cook, and I sure hope I am spoiling you. That's what I'm here for! I want you to think of nothing but me."

We had an early dinner, and I fed Mya and Shadow and took them out while Zack cleaned up the dishes. When I came in, he was sitting on the couch flipping through the TV channels. "Do you want to go anywhere? The movies, maybe?" he asked.

"No, I'd rather stay home. I'm a kind of homebody and with the new pups and a full week of work again, I just want to relax here...if that's ok with you."

HEARTS BLAZING

"Hey, anything you want to do is fine with me. I have to tell you Tara I really like you. I am so glad I met you. I know I told you that before, but I just wanted to tell you again."

"Thanks, I like you too."

We just sat around watching TV until around ten o'clock. Then Zack said he'd better leave. He had an early day tomorrow, and he knew I was starting my job of going to sit with Alice. So we said our goodbyes. He said he'd be over around six, and he did his usual of waving and beeping as he drove away.

The next morning I arrived at Alice's at noon with Mya and Shadow in tow. "Well hello!" she said as she opened the door. "Oh my gosh, look at these beautiful little creatures. Give me one!" I handed Mya to her as I went and put the groceries in the kitchen. It was just after twelve so I asked Alice if she wanted me to make her a sandwich and a cup of tea. "Oh that would be lovely, bring the other pup in here with me to watch, I can't get over how beautiful they are." I brought Shadow in the front room and built a sort of little pen on the floor for them.

"I just fed them and took them out right before coming here so they should be ok," I told her. I went back in the kitchen and made a sandwich and cup of tea for Alice. She seemed like such a nice lady. I knew I was going to love this job. I would really be busy now, with this job, my cleanings, and of course Zach, who had seemed to become a permanent fixture in my house over the last few days. He really was a nice man though, and I did like him. It was nice to have someone over at night to watch TV with.

I went back in the front room and gave Alice her lunch. We sat and talked for hours just getting to know each other. Her daughter lived in Arizona with her husband and two children. She had a son who lived in Washington. He wasn't married. He had been through a bad divorce and said he never wanted to go down that road again. Her husband had died some twenty years ago. They had been

31

together since they were in high school. She thought she would never find another man like him so she never tried. She talked about how she really needed some painting done around the house and just never trusted anyone to do it. I told her maybe I could do it. I painted the rooms in my house. "Oh I don't want you to do it, I just want you to come and sit with me, do some laundry and make me tea. That's my favorite. Tell me about you now dear." I went on to tell her I, like her son, was divorced, but I worked so much that I never really had time to meet anyone else. Plus I really didn't know if I wanted to go down that road again either. I told her about Zack and how I met him. "Well he seems like he'd be gone for you," she replied.

"Yeah he is, and we seem to have a good time together."

We talked about what a lover of wolves I was and how I got the two pups. Then we talked about how I needed someone to remodel me kitchen. "Oh I hate it so much, I've hated it since I moved into the house. It was so ugly. But everything took money," I told her, "and like you, I don't trust anyone to do it either."

Before we knew it my three hours with Alice were over. "I can't wait for tomorrow for you to come back again. I had fun talking to you," she said.

"Now tomorrow when I come back I'll do your laundry so have it ready and you can watch Mya and Shadow."

"I think we're going to make a wonderful pair."

"Me too, call me if you need anything." I picked up Mya and Shadow and put them in the car. We got home and I had a pile of mail. Then I remembered I had never even gotten my mail on Saturday. After feeding the pups and taking them out, I went and took a shower. Then I went and sat down on the couch and finally started going through the mail. I looked at the clock and it was already five thirty. I had to get dressed and ready; Zack would be here pretty soon. It was ten minutes to six when he showed up. "Did you eat?" I asked, I remembered we had the leftovers from last night.

HEARTS BLAZING

"Yeah, I grabbed a sandwich at home. What a day, I'm beat!"

"Well I'm going to go heat up the food from yesterday and we could eat that. I'm going to whip up a cake too."

"Don't go to any trouble for me. I'm sure you had a long day too."

"It's no trouble I want to."

I went in the kitchen and yelled for Zack to just put the TV on. When I came back in the front room Zack was asleep on the couch. I looked at him and smiled. I pulled a blanket over him and just let him sleep. He must have had a really hard day.

About an hour had passed when he woke up. I was in the kitchen frosting the cake when he came up behind me and kissed my neck. "You are a beautiful woman," he said. "I'm sorry I fell asleep."

"Hey it's ok; you were tired."

"Well I don't ever want you to be mad at me."

"How could I be mad that you worked so hard you needed some extra rest"?

"Well come on let me make it up to you. Dance with me." He put the radio on, took me in his arms, and started twirling me around. He laughed and made faces at me. I laughed back and told him he was crazy. I hadn't had this much fun in ages. When the song was over a slow song came on and he drew me close. He rubbed my back and whispered in my ear, "Tara I love you."

I pulled away in shock. We hadn't even known each other a week. He saw the look on my face and said, "I'm sorry I didn't mean to upset you. I just…. I just can't get you out of my mind. I can give you a nice life if you'd just give me a chance. I could provide a nice life for you and protect you. You wouldn't have to work so hard. I want to marry you. I don't want to lose what we have together. I promise to make you happy until the day I die."

I was stunned. I didn't know what to say. We didn't even know each other. I did like him and had fun with him, but love…that was another thought. I just stood there, at a loss for words.

33

TINA VELAZQUEZ

"I can see you're shocked, you don't have to answer yet, just think about it and tell me your answer when you're ready. Just remember all I've said to you. I am a good guy. I'd never hurt you. You'd never want for anything. If you don't love me that's ok; maybe one day you would. I love you Tara. I think I fell in love with you the first moment I saw you. I'll even get your kitchen fixed. Whatever you want. Give me a chance to make your life happy again. I've never felt this way about anyone else. I never even came close to asking anyone to marry me."

"Zack I don't know what to say."

"Don't say anything. Lets just have some of that cake you were frosting and watch the news, yeah"?

"Ok go put it on I'll be right there," I managed to spit out.

I went to the kitchen and got the cake in shock. I felt like I'd just waken from a dream. I came back with the cake and we just watched the news. I started yawning and Zack said he better get going so I could get some sleep. He took me in his arms before he walked out the door and told me to at least think about what he had asked me. I told him I would. We kissed good night and he went running down the walkway. When he got just to the end he turned around jumping in the air and yelled "Tara I Love You, I do, I do, I do. Sleep tight."

I laughed and waved. He seemed like a little kid. He beeped as he drove away. About forty-five minutes later the phone rang. I had just gotten into bed. Who could that be at this hour I thought. "Hello?"

"Sweet dreams, sweetheart, I forgot to tell you. I love you. Please tell me you'll marry me soon…"

"Oh Zack, you said you'd give me some time."

"I will. Just wishful thinking I guess. I hope your answer will come in your dreams tonight and you'll call me with a yes tomorrow. "

"We'll see."

34

HEARTS BLAZING

"I guess I'll have to settle for that for now my love, good night."

"Good night Zack."

I went to sleep with my mind in a whirl of everything Zack had said to me. Should I give marriage another try? I wasn't getting any younger. I was always working so I had no time to ever go out and meet anyone. Could I grow to love him? Could I at least care enough about him to share my life? I did have fun with him. He did have the most gorgeous eyes I had ever seen. But was that enough? Was that enough to keep me happy? I didn't want to hurt him. What should I do? I fell asleep wondering.

Chapter 7

I woke the next morning and did my usual routine with Mya and Shadow. I didn't have to be at Alice's until noon, but I wanted to stop and get her a candy bar. I wrapped a piece of cake for her, then I wrapped the pups and went to the store. I arrived at Alice's a little before noon. She opened the door, all smiles, and said, "Give me the little ones. Oh, they're sleeping! We must be quiet." She went in the house and put them down on a big comforter on the floor that she told me she had found last night. She didn't use it anymore so she was giving it to her new little babies. I laughed and handed her the chocolate candy bar and the piece of chocolate cake I had brought her.

"Sweets for the sweet lady," I said.

"Oh my goodness I can see we're really going to get along well. Thank-you so much sweetheart."

"Oh you're very welcome. It's the least I can do since you're so sweet."

I went to make her a cup of tea to go with her cake. When she sat at the table I told her to start eating her cake and while I put her laundry in the washer and then we'd talk.

"Ok sweetheart. It's in the bathroom. I'll be good while you're gone and don't worry about the little ones. If they wake up, I'll get them."

"I'm sure you will, I laughed."

36

HEARTS BLAZING

I went downstairs and put Alice's clothes in the washer. She had a huge basement that looked like it had seen a party or two in previous years. When I came upstairs I told Alice what a nice basement she had.

"Oh we had many a party there when my husband and I were young.'"?

"I thought so. I noticed all the hanging lights and the bar from one wall to another."

"Yeah that seems like such a long time ago but in my mind it feels like yesterday. I can relive things that were said and people that were here. We had many good times down there. I'll always remember." She sat there starring with this far away look in her eyes. She looked so at peace and so happy I knew she was reliving those days and I knew her and her husband had a happy marriage. I knew she was remembering him.

Could I have that with Zack I wondered? Could I be happy even though I didn't love him?

"My dear what are you thinking of? You look so far in thought," Alice asked.

"Oh, it's Zack. He was over last night and he asked me to marry him."

"Oh my goodness. What did you say?"

"I told him he was moving too fast. I hardly even know him that well."

"Well what are you going to do?"?

"I don't know. He is a nice man. I have fun with him. He really has spoiled me since I've known him. I think I can get used to that, but is that enough for marriage?" I asked.

"Let me tell you something sweetheart. Sometimes a woman stays with a man she doesn't love. Maybe it's to prevent loneliness. Sometimes there is love, but love isn't enough. Sometimes you have to take a chance. It's just something for you to think of honey. You're young yet. You don't want to be alone like me. I had a very good life with my husband. We were together very young. We had good times and bad, but we loved each other very much. We were fortunate. Some people never have that. I miss him so much at times my heart aches. I just want to die so I can be with him again. Now at my age, of course, I would never want to be with anyone else. My husband was my life. I still tell him goodnight every night before I go to sleep. I know you probably think that's strange, but to me, in the dark, it feels like he's still with me right beside me. But you're still so young and you have so much life to give someone. In fact I was thinking of this last night. I know you're really busy, but I would love for you to come here everyday instead of three times a week. Even if the other free days you're only here for one or two hours. You lift my spirits. You make me feel young again. Of course, you could be off on Sundays. That would be your and Zack's day. Then I'd get to see Mya and Shadow everyday. I'll even pay you more. Whatever you want."

I really liked Alice and I could spare a few hours everyday even on Sundays so I told her yes. She sat there clapping her hands with tears in her eyes. I was happy and so was she. Before we knew it the day was over again. I told her I'd be back tomorrow, but it would probably be after noon since I had four cleanings I did on Wednesdays. "I'll get here around two and stay until five."

"That would be fine my dear."

I loaded the pups in the car and drove home. When I got up to the door I noticed some kind of wrapped package. I didn't order anything. As I got closer I noticed a card on top so I opened the door, put the pups down and went out to get the package. I opened the card; "To my beautiful lady who I hope will be my Wife, love Zack."

What did this man do now? Hasn't he brought me enough food? I opened the package and inside was a little teddy bear with blue eyes that said "I Love You." Then there was a little basket of all kinds

HEARTS BLAZING

of bath bubbles and soaps. "Boy," I thought, "this man is making it really hard to say single. He seems to know all the right things to do."

I went over and fed the pups. While they were eating I called Zack to tell him thank-you.

"Hello," he said.

"Hi I just wanted to call and tell you thank-you for yet another gift."

"What do you mean? That's the first thing I ever bought you."

"Oh come on now! How much food have you brought over?"

"That's not a gift. You have to eat don't you? Plus I ate half that food too. Speaking of food, what do you want me to pick you up for dinner? How about Chinese tonight?"

"Zack, you don't have to bring food every night."

"I know I don't have to bring food every night. I want to. Don't you want to snuggle with me and watch TV? You don't want me over? Oh please tell me that's not true."

He acted like he was crying. I started laughing, "Oh stop it of course you can come over, but you can't stay late. I have a really busy day tomorrow."

"Ok I'll be there within the hour with the food. You supply the plates and drink and we'll be set.

"Ok you win."

"All I want to win now is your hand in marriage. That would be the best win ever."

"Ha, ha," was all that would come out. "See you in a bit."

I took Mya and Shadow out. When I came in I decided to make ice tea. As I was getting the plates together and putting ice in the glasses I heard the front door open and then Zack's voice. "Dinner is served madam." I went in the front room and there was Zack, two bags in each hand.

"Hey, come on in the kitchen. I just made some ice tea," I said. We sat and ate and talked about our day. I told him about how I was

39

TINA VELAZQUEZ

going to sit with Alice everyday instead of just three days a week. "She is such a sweet little lady. Just lonely I guess. She loves Mya and Shadow too."

We finished eating and cleaned the kitchen. Then we went in to watch TV. We both fell asleep on the couch and when I woke up, it was three in the morning. The TV was still on. I didn't have the heart to wake Zack. He looked so peaceful. As I looked at him I thought, "You know I could get used to waking up with this man beside me everyday." I put a blanket over him and I went into the bedroom.

Chapter 8

I woke to the pups' whimpering sounds. They had been sleeping since eight o'clock the night before. They hadn't even gone out before bed. I jumped out of bed and threw on a pair of pants and shirt so I could take them out. It was eight o'clock already and my first appointment was at nine. When we got back in the house I remembered Zack had fallen asleep on the couch. I went in the front room to wake him, but to my surprise, he was gone. There was a little bag on the table and a note, "Good morning my love. I had an early start today and didn't want to wake you so enjoy your breakfast and I'll be over tonight. I LOVE YOU! LOVE ZACK." I opened the bag and in it were a cup of coffee and two donuts. This man was too much I thought. Either that or he thinks I'm really skinny. I took a sip of the coffee and went and got dressed.

When I came out the pups were done eating so I took them out again and then put them in their pen. I told them I'd be back for them to take them to Alice's, but in the meantime to be my little angels. This was the first day they were really going to be alone for such an extended length of time. I made sure all of their toys and blankets were with them. I grabbed my coffee and bag of donuts and was out the door.

When I got to Millie's house she was standing in the door. "Well hello my dear. I was checking for mail."

"Hi Millie! How are you today?"

41

"Oh fine, just like always I guess."

We went into the house and I brought my cleaning things into the kitchen. She started, "Well, come on. What went on with you since you were here last?" There she was, sitting there with that smile on her face, and I knew she was going to start up with the whole dating thing. Every Monday was the same. She'd sit at the table and ask me that same question. Then she'd go on to say I should date...at least on the weekends.

"Well let's see, I adopted, or should I say bought, two wolf hybrid puppies and I met this guy named Zack. And I've been with him every night since last Monday."

"What? You're just saying that! You think I'm going to start asking you about dating my nephew."

"No, I'm serious. I met him at Martha's house last week. You know Martha. He was over there fixing her door and we started talking. The next thing I knew, he was coming over bringing me food every night."

"Oh I'm so happy for you. See, I told you that you needed a nice man in your life."

"Yeah, he is nice."

"Now, what about these wolves? Aren't you afraid of them?"

"Of course not! They are the cutest little creatures. You know that I'm such a big lover of wolves. I went into the store and there was this sign up from someone that was selling them. I called, went out to see them, and feel in love with them on the spot."

"Oh, nothing you do surprises me, Tara. I wish you luck with them. Not that you need any...and with this Zack guy too."

"Thanks, now on that note I better get to work." I went about cleaning Millie's house. She came in the room I was in and told me how she went to bingo on Wednesday and won one hundred dollars.

"I was so shocked I couldn't believe it. So you know what that means?"

HEARTS BLAZING

"You're going again this week?" I asked.

"No, you're going to get a better tip today! I'll pay for some food for these little wolves of yours. By the way, what did you name them?"

I told her I named one Shadow because she was always hiding behind her sister and the other one Mya. She had really blue eyes. Then I told her about Zack's blue eyes and how they were the first thing I noticed about him.

Millie said, "Well I guess my nephew is out of luck then. Too bad You would have been good for him."

"Yeah, yeah...you're always trying to get me to go out with someone. Well, now I am, so there! Oh, and I haven't even told you what he asked me!"

"What? Don't leave me hanging!"

"He asked me to marry him!"

"What? And you've only known him a week"? She sat there with her mouth open and her hand on her chest. Then she started laughing.

"What?" was all I could say.

"Well, you haven't dated in years and now you go out with a guy for a week and he's already popped the question! You must have really impressed him."

"I don't know about that. He's never been married and he's forty-four years old. Maybe he doesn't want to die an old man alone," I laughed.

"Well, what was your answer"?

"I told him it's too fast."

"Is it? Or are you just too scared to go down that route again?"

"I don't really know. I wish I did." We sat there just looking at each other. "Well I'm done and I better get going on to the next job. I have three more cleanings to do and then I go to this lady's house everyday and sit with her. She lets me bring Mya and Shadow."

"Oh that's sweet. Well, here my dear." Millie gave me my pay and a nice tip. I told her I'd see her next week, same time same place. She wished me good luck in everything and I walked down the stairs. It was a little before eleven when I got to Mary's house. I knocked and walked in as usual. "Hi Mary."

"Hi Tara."

I began, "Well before you start about your grandson, let me tell you...I have a boyfriend now and I also bought two wolf hybrid puppies last week."

"Wait, one shock at a time for this old lady," she laughed. I went on to tell her the same story I just told Millie.

"Oh, I'm so happy for you. Now you won't just have work to do. You'll have a husband to take care of!"

"Now wait a minute; I didn't say anything about a husband to take care of. I said he asked me to marry him. Don't you think it's a little too soon for that?"

"My dear, listen to an old lady. Life is short, too short sometimes, and good men are hard to find. They are so far and few in between. So if you seem to get along and you enjoy each other, follow what your mind tells you to do. You can grow to love him someday maybe and if not, at least you're not alone. You even told me one time not to long ago that it's hard for you to meet anyone with the way you're always working, so maybe this man was sent to you."

"I don't know. I always believed you married for love."

"That too sweetheart, but sometimes maybe there's something else in store for us."

"Yeah, well I'll give everything you said to me some thought. It just feels like there'd be something missing." I told Mary I better start cleaning or I'd never get through my day. When I was done I bid my farewell and was on my way.

Next I pulled up to Martha's house. She was standing in front, watering her pots of Marigolds. "Well Tara, you're right on time as usual. Let's go in. I was just watering my flowers. It's so hot out

HEARTS BLAZING

today," she greeted me. We went in the house and I brought my cleaning things in the kitchen. "So tell me, did anything come of you and Zack? You seemed to have hit it off well here last week."?

"Oh, let me tell you. I think you should sit down. Yes, I've been seeing Zack since I left here last week, and on Monday he asked me to marry him!"

"What! What did you just say?" I told her the same story again. I told her things were moving way too fast for me. "Well what are you going to do?" she questioned.

I told her I didn't know. "I do like him, but marriage? That's a whole different thing." Martha just sat there and said nothing. "Are you ok?" I asked.

"Yes, I'm just shocked."

"You and me both, but I guess we'll get through it right?" We both started laughing.

"Yeah, and to think it all started here at this house. You don't even date and you go and get yourself a marriage proposal," Martha said.

"I kind of feel giddy in a way. I don't know why."

Martha laughed, "Oh, you're probably loving it and you know it. You'll get over the shock soon."

We both laughed and I told her I better start cleaning. I told her I had one more house to do and then I go to sit with a lady for a few hours a day just to keep her company.

"Ok, go ahead honey. I won't keep you anymore. Besides I have to digest everything you just told me. I can tell you though, I've known Zack for a while, and he is a good man. He's done a few jobs for me and a few of my lady friends, and he is very nice."

"Oh I know he is, but I'm not sure if that's enough to marry him."

"Well, that's only for you to decide. No one else can make that decision."

I went in the bathroom to start cleaning. Boy, what was my decision going to be? The more I thought about it, the more I thought

45

I'd say yes. Was that crazy? He was a good guy. I wasn't getting any younger and I never had the time to meet anyone anyway. Besides wasn't love overrated?

I finished up at Martha's and said my goodbyes. On I went to Jill's house, my last cleaning of the day before Alice's. I sure hoped Mya and Shadow were ok. About an hour and a half more and I'd be able to go get them. I pulled up in front of Jill's and got my cleaning things out of the trunk. I rang the bell and Jill answered right away. "Hi are you feeling better?" I asked her.

"Oh yes, my dear. I feel much better. I think it was just something I ate that day."

"Oh, I'm glad to hear that," I said as I walked into the house. "Boy, do I have something to tell you."

"It must be something good, the way you're talking," Jill smiled.

"Well you know how I told you I always loved wolves?"

"Yeah, you always have a shirt on with a picture of a wolf when you clean. If I remember, you have a picture of a wolf on your business card too."

"Bingo! Only now I'll have to get new cards with two wolves on it."

She looked at me with a kind of stunned look. "Why…you're not getting a helper are you"?

"Oh no, not that, but… I bought two wolf hybrid puppies last week!"

"You what? Where? How?"

I went on to tell her the story. The whole time she sat with her hands clapped in front of her, looking so surprised. "I can't believe it! You never cease to amaze me with the things you do my dear."

"I know. I sort of surprised myself. It's not like I planned on getting them. It just sort of happened. They are so adorable, though. You couldn't even imagine."

"I'm sure they are, and I'm sure you spoil them rotten."

"No, now why would I do that?" I laughed as I was filling my bucket with water.

I went to start my cleaning routine and noticed a box of chocolates on the table next to the TV. "I see you treated yourself to a box of chocolates, Jill."

"No, actually a man at the senior group I belong to gave them to me."

Now it was my time to look shocked. "Well, well…you've been holding out on me…not telling me your little secrets!"

"No, oh heavens no…" she stopped talking as if to think of what to say. Then she finished, "Well I don't know. He asked me to go out to dinner with him after he gave me them."

"Oh boy, now I'm shocked!" I gave her a smile. "Are you going?"

"Well yeah, I think so. It's totally innocent."

"You should. I think it would be nice for you to get out." Then I told her about Zack.

"Oh you're just full of surprises today," she said.

"Look who's talking?" I laughed.

I was done cleaning so I told Jill to have fun at dinner and left to go home for Mya and Shadow. When I walked in the door they were so happy to see me. They started yipping and running around in circles. "Ok, ok! Mommy's home. Lets go out."

I looked at the clock and it was one-twenty so I had time to feed the little ones before going to Alice's. We got back in the house and I had a cup of tea while they were eating. Twenty minutes later, with them and their bag of toys in tow, we were back in the car.

Alice was opening the door when I pulled up. "Come on, hurry. Bring in my little babies."

"You weren't waiting for them were you?" I asked.

"What do you think? This is the hi-light of my day." We all went in the house and Alice held out her hands and talked to Mya and Shadow as they licked her face, making her laugh. I had never seen her so happy.

"Do you need to go to the store today? We could leave the pups.

They just ate so you know they'll go to sleep for awhile to take a nap."

"Yeah, we could do that. Could you take me to the drug store, too? You know the one right by the store?"

"Sure, that's no problem at all. Want some tea first though while you're playing with your babies?"

"Yes, of course I'll say yes to that!"

I went in to make her tea and got her a plate of cookies since I knew she liked her sweets. It was already five o'clock when we got back from running Alice's errands so I brought her groceries in, unpacked them, and told her I'd be back tomorrow. By the time I got home it was already going on six o'clock. I brought Mya and Shadow in the house and fed them. I put on a kettle of water for tea before taking them out. When we came back in, the doorbell rang. It was Zack.

"Hey there," he said in his usual cheerful voice.

"Hi, I just got home."

"You're kidding! You had quite a long day. Why don't you get your tea and come sit on the couch? I'll massage your back."

"Can I go take a quick shower first?"

"Sure, take a long one if you want. I'm not going anywhere."

I went in and took a shower. The warm water felt so good on my body after such a long day. I loved my jobs, but sometimes I just wished I was really rich and didn't have to work. I had to admit, I was really tired today for some reason. Not that I'd admit that to anyone but myself.

Zack had the news on when I got in the front room. "Here you go sweetheart. I brought your tea."

"You think of everything, thanks." He massaged my shoulders while I drank my tea. His hands felt so good and strong. I felt myself almost falling asleep.

"I don't want to pressure you or anything Tara, but have you

HEARTS BLAZING

thought at all about an answer to my question? I could make your life so much easier for you. You wouldn't have to even work if you didn't want to."

I thought for a minute and then, like it wasn't even my own voice, I said, "Yes, I'll marry you."

He hugged me and kissed me and told me I'd made him the happiest man in the world. I myself was shocked because I wasn't sure how those words even came out of my mouth. I hugged him back though and we lay back on the couch, his arms around me, and watched TV.

"You won't regret this decision, Tara. I promise you I will be the best provider and husband anyone could ever want or need. You will never want for anything ever. Thank you for making me so happy. I love you."

At around eleven o'clock I told him I didn't want to be rude, but I really needed some sleep. "I have to get these pups out, too, before they go to sleep."

"Yeah they are a lot of work for you."

"No they're not. I love them and they're so cute!"

"Yeah I guess," was all he said. He got up and I told him I'd see him tomorrow.

I watched him leave and then I went to take the little ones out. "How could he not like you two?" I was thinking. He didn't seem like much of an animal lover like I was. That didn't sit too well with me. We went in the house and the three of us fell fast asleep, almost immediately.

49

Chapter 9

Gosh, I couldn't believe Thursday had arrived already. I just have Helen and June today, I thought to myself as I was getting ready for work. Of course I had Alice too, but she was such a joy to be around I didn't even call her work. Then again all my clients were a joy to be around.

The morning went by fast. Nothing too interesting happened to either June or Helen since I last cleaned. Of course they both wanted to know about Zack. But they also wanted to hear about Mya and Shadow too. They were the first I told about Zack's marriage proposal.

Helen was so happy that she jumped for joy! And, of course, June clutched her heart again like she was going to faint. "You should have been in the movies June. You missed your calling, that's for sure."

When I got to Alice's house at noon, after picking up Mya and Shadow, she was waiting at the door. "Let me see my babies. I've been waiting all morning," she said.

I handed her the pups and showed her what I stopped to get her on my way over.

"Oh goody! A candy bar! You sure know how to please an old lady." ?

"Let me go get your tea. Then we'll talk. Do I have news to tell you today!"

HEARTS BLAZING

"Oh sounds important! Hurry back!"

I went in the kitchen and got her a sandwich and chips with her tea. I made myself a cup too. When I got back to the front room I couldn't believe my eyes. There on the floor was Alice playing with Mya and Shadow.

"They sure have made you young again! Look at you down there on the floor! When I first started coming here you were acting like you were at death's door. Now you're on the floor and you didn't even fall!"

We both laughed until tears were in our eyes. I helped Alice up and put a tray by her chair with her lunch on it. The pups were falling asleep.

"Tell me your news. I can't wait," Alice said.

I told her about Zack's proposal and that I had said yes. I had some mixed feelings about it, but I knew he was a good man. "We're talking about seven months from now. Valentines Day actually."

"I'm so happy for you. You will stay with me though, won't you?"

"Of course. I'd never even consider leaving you. You'd have to kick me down the stairs and drag me to my car to get rid of me!"

She laughed. "Oh come on now… I'd never do that."

"I know. You're too sweet. Besides, how could I take your grand puppies from you?"

As soon as I said that, Mya gave out her first little howl and Shadow tried to copy.

"Oh my goodness, they're howling like wolves!" Alice said. We both tried to howl with them. Then, as fast as they did the howling they both fell fast asleep.

"I really love these little guys so much," Alice said.

"I would have never in my dreams thought I would have ever had one either," I told her. "But now that I do I couldn't imagine my life without them."

"Yes my dear, you have two for double the pleasure. I am so

happy to have met you and brought you into my life. Or should I say that you wanted to be here. I would have still been so lonely and I would have never met them. Thank you so much Tara," Alice said as tears filled her eyes.

"You are more than welcome. I also love the time we are able to spend together. I'm glad I'm able to help."

"Oh, I forgot to tell you! When you're here tomorrow, I have a man coming over to give me a price for painting the house and maybe redoing the bathroom. He's the grandson of a friend of mine and he remodels homes that are in need of repair. She says he knows how to do everything and he'll give me a good price because I'm a friend of hers. Maybe you could talk to him about your kitchen."

"Yeah well, I'd have to win the lottery by tomorrow then."

"The only thing is that he works at another job during the day, so he'll have to come at night to do the work. I was going to ask you if you could come in the evening while he's working here, maybe just three days a week?"

"Sure I don't see why not."

"Oh good, then I guess we'll meet him tomorrow."

"That we will! My goodness, I just noticed it's already three o'clock, so I'm going to get going. I'll be here by noon tomorrow. I can't believe it's already Friday!"

"Take care of my babies tonight," Alice said.

"Oh you know I will." I waved as I got in the car.

I parked in front of the house, took Mya and Shadow out of the backseat, picked up my mail and went inside. "Come on little ones, you have to go out before you eat."

They yipped as they ran out the back door. They were getting pretty smart; they'd already figured out the routine. I looked over and saw the light blinking on the answering machine. The message was from Zack. He was having a problem on a job so he wouldn't be able to make it over tonight. He said he'd call before I went to

HEARTS BLAZING

sleep to say goodnight. Unless, that is, I wanted him to come spend the night when he finished with work. Otherwise he'd talk to me later. It'll be nice to have an early night for a change. As far as calling him back to stay the night, that wasn't going to happen. The pups were usually asleep by nine, so that's when I'd turn in too. I was really beat this week for some reason, so I was kind of glad Zack wasn't coming over.

Chapter 10

On Friday morning I woke to the pups scampering around in their pen. Oh my gosh, I thought to myself, I must have fallen asleep as soon as I laid down last night. The sun was streaming through the bedroom window. "Ok little ones! I'm up! Let's go outside."

I reached over to pick them up and they started licking my hands. "I know you're hungry, but outside first."

When we came back in and after I fed them, I decided to have some toast with my coffee. I was so tired last night I didn't even eat.

The phone started ringing as my toast popped up. It was Zack.

"Hey what happened to you last night? I called you around ten and there was no answer. I left a message. Didn't you get it? You never called me back. I was worried!"

"Oh Zack, I haven't even checked my machine. I was so tired I fell asleep as soon as I put Mya and Shadow down for the night."

"That's ok. I was just worried. I almost came over to check on you. Well, I'll be over tonight. I finally finished that job about nine-thirty last night. What a mess! People should let the pros do what they do best instead of trying to do things themselves just to save some money."

He sounded really angry.

"Yeah, well you know, sometimes people don't have the money."

"Yeah well… I'll bring dinner so don't worry. Love you."

HEARTS BLAZING

"Yeah me too." As I hung up the phone, I thought about how angry he sounded. He never even asked about Mya and Shadow. He never seemed interested in them. What will happen when we get married? It's coming up right around the corner. I sure wish I could be one hundred percent sure of this. It just felt like something was missing.

I got to Alice's about ten minutes before noon. She was all smiles as usual. "Hello my dear! I have the laundry all ready for you to put in the washer after you get my tea! And remember Jonathon will be here today. Probably around two o'clock."

"No problem!" I told her. I headed into the house to make lunch and throw the clothes in the washer while she played with her grand pups.

At two fifteen the doorbell rang. I answered the door.

"Hi I'm here to see Alice. My name's Jonathon."

"Sure, come in. She's in the front room."

He walked in the front room and the pups started yipping. "Wow! What do we have here? You two look like wolves!" He was laughing and picking them up. They were licking him and scampering like he was a long lost friend.

"They really like you," I said. "You're right too, they are sort of wolves. They're wolf hybrid pups. They're half timber wolf and half Husky."

"What are their names?"

"Mya and Shadow. They're both girls," I told him.

"They're really cute. How old?" he asked. He was laughing and wrestling with them on the floor. He looked like a natural.

"They're about three months. I just got them a few weeks ago."

"Wow! You're really lucky," he said. "I could play with these little guys all day."

I watched him and laughed. I thought to myself how much different he was with them than Zack.

55

"Their my grand pups," Alice said. "Tara brings them with her everyday."

"Oh I'm sorry! We got so caught up in the pups I forgot to introduce you to Alice, the lady you came to see!"

"Hi Alice," he said. "I guess that makes you Tara?"

"Yes, that's me."

"Tara is my personal helper. She's here six days a week, so get used to seeing her and the pups," Alice said.

He winked at me and said, "Oh believe me, I think I can get used to seeing them all really easy."

I just smiled.

"Alice, do you want me to show Jonathan what you want done?"

"Yes, that would be nice my dear. I'll just sit with the little ones. They look like you tired them out Jonathan."

"Yeah it looks like nap time, but I'll definitely be back to see you both." He smiled at the pups and rubbed their heads.

He had a nice smile. He seemed really nice too. I showed him all the rooms she wanted painted and the bathroom she wanted remodeled.

"She wants everything gutted in here right?" he asked.

"Yep she wants all new."

"No problem. Let me go sit down and figure out a price." ?We went back in the front room where we found Mya and Shadow sleeping.

"It's a mess right?" Alice asked.

"No it's not too bad. I can have it all fixed up for you. You do know though that I'll have to come after five o'clock though, because I have my regular job during the day."

"That's no problem. I really don't go anywhere except to the store with Tara and that's in the afternoon."

"And here's what everything would cost." He handed her a piece of paper.

HEARTS BLAZING

"That's just fine. I thought it would be more. See Tara, you should have him look at your kitchen. It might not be as much as you think."

"Yeah I just have a lack of money right now though."

"Well when you get ready, remember me," he winked again.

"Oh I will," I said. Now what made me say that? It sounded like I was flirting with him... and maybe I was.

We said our goodbyes and he said he could start on the job tomorrow. He could be there around noon since he didn't work on Saturdays.

"That would be fine," Alice said. "Tara will be here with her pups too."

"Well I look forward to seeing her and her pups."

I felt kind of funny inside. It seemed like he was looking right through me. He whispered goodbye to Mya and Shadow quietly because he said he didn't want to wake them.

"Wow, I really love these little ones," he said. "I can't believe they're half wolf."

And I can't believe how interested he is in them, I thought. This is my kind of guy... Oh now what made me think that? I'm supposed to be getting married in six months!

Chapter 11

I got home around four and did the routine of taking the pups out, feeding them, then bringing them in and making tea.

At a few minutes to six the doorbell rang. It was Zack with his arms full as usual; only this time there was a red rose on top.

"Brought enough for an army again I see."

"Well hello to you too," he said. He kissed my cheek as he walked in the door. We went in and sat down to eat. We each talked about our day and I told him about Jonathan and how delighted he was with the wolves.

"Think of all the fur they're going to shed when they get bigger," was his only response.

"You don't like them do you?" I asked.

"I didn't say that."

"You didn't have to."

We were silent while we finished eating. I couldn't understand how anyone couldn't like my little pups. They were beautiful. He was being such a jerk! What have I gotten myself into?

After watching a few TV shows I told Zack I was really tired and asked if he would mind leaving so I could go to sleep.

"I know you're tired, but you're mad at me too."

I didn't answer. I just got up off the couch. I felt like saying, "Love me… love my wolves. Oh and by the way, I made a mistake. I don't want to marry you." But I didn't. I shut the door as soon as he

HEARTS BLAZING

stepped out. I didn't even watch him drive away.

After he left I took Mya and Shadow outside. I put them down in my bedroom on the floor in their blanket. "I love you guys," I said as I kissed the tops of their heads. I thought how revolted Zack would be at the sight of that and how Jonathan would smile at me.

I was so happy to be living somewhere where I could have these two. I had about five acres of land, but I knew when they got bigger they would need a little, or should I say big, pen outside. This old farmhouse had been in the family for years and although it needed some work, it was ok.

The one problem Zack and I had, beside him not liking the pups, was that he wanted me to move into his house when we got married. He lived in the next town, not far from me, but I don't think my babies would be welcome there. I wasn't about to give them up.

I went to sleep that night in a fit of restlessness. It seemed like I was tossing and turning all night and I woke up just as tired as when I went to bed.

Chapter 12

When I made it over to Alice's at noon, I was still upset about how Zack talked about my little ones. I told Alice about it.

"Well phooey on him. I don't even know him and I don't like him. How could anyone not like these little ones?"

"I don't know," I said. "I'm going to go get us each a cup of tea. Jonathan should be here pretty soon."

The doorbell rang right at one o'clock. "Hey I hoped you'd be here already. You did bring my new friends didn't you?" Jonathan walked in the house and immediately got on his knees. He started talking in baby talk to the pups and kissed both of them. "Look what I got for you both?" He pulled out two bones. "Can I give them each one?" he asked.

"Sure!" I told him. I couldn't believe he cared enough to bring them bones! They were jumping all over him to grab them. Once they got them they both settled down and started chewing them like there was no tomorrow.

"Well, let me go get my stuff out of the truck."

"I'll help you. Do you have a lot to bring in?"

"Not really. Just some drop cloths, ladder, brushes, scrappers, rags, primer and paint."

"All right," I laughed, "you need help. Come on."

Alice smiled as we walked out the door.

Before we knew it the day had flown by. It was eight o'clock in

60

the evening. I had made Alice dinner around four o'clock and of course I had stayed way longer than my usual four hours. I lost track of time. I hadn't had so much fun and enjoyed talking to someone as much as I did Jonathan. He was a great guy and he made me laugh a lot.

We worked in Alice's bedroom getting it ready to paint all day, but we also took the pups out in the yard a few times and played with them.

We cleaned everything up. I told Alice I'd see her Monday. Jonathan said he was going to be there the next day, Sunday, to continue what we started.

"Hey, you want to come tomorrow and help me again?" he asked. "I'll pay you and even bring more bones."

It didn't take me long to say yes.

When I got home I showered and the three of us went to bed. I didn't even think of Zack. I really couldn't wait until tomorrow to see Jonathan again.

The next day was another good day. So were the next few months. I didn't see much of Zack. I spent a lot of time at Alice's, both during the day and at night with Jonathan. I went to my other cleaning jobs too, but always looked forward to going to Alice's the most.

One Thursday after cleaning at Helen and June's, Alice greeted me outside when I pulled up to her house. She couldn't hold the pups anymore; they were getting too big. They jumped all around her when they got in the house though. Good thing her house was huge! When I brought her out her lunch, I started humming a song that was in my head all day.

"I have to tell you Tara, you seem so much happier these past few months. It doesn't happen to have anything to do with a certain someone named Jonathan does it?" she smiled.

"As much as it shouldn't, yes I think it does."

"Oh my! What are you going to do about Zack? You can't avoid him forever you know!"

"I know. I just don't know what to say. How do you tell the man you're supposed to marry that you're really in love with someone else?" My mouth gasped open. "Oh my gosh! I'm in love. I mean... I'm really in love. I'm in love with Jonathan! I don't love Zack. I never really did. I was in love with the idea of being in love. What am I going to do?"

"My dear, you have to follow your heart. I see the way you and Jonathan look at each other. I saw it the first day you two laid eyes on one another. I see the way you are together. I hear how he makes you laugh when you are in the other room helping him. He loves you too!"

"How do you know that? He told you?"

"My dear, I may be an old lady, but I'm not blind. He doesn't need to tell me anything. I can see the way he looks at you. The way his eyes sparkle when he talks to you."

"Oh Alice, I'm staying here with you tonight if that's ok. I can't go home. I need to clear my head. I need some time to myself to think."

"Well here comes Jonathan up the walk, so you better not start crying."

My heart started to flutter when he walked in the door.

"Hey," he went right to Mya and Shadow with bones in hand. "Hi Tara... Alice, how's the day going girls?"

"Good I guess," I said. "I can't believe it's this late already."

"Yeah I know. I haven't even eaten yet," he said. "How about going with me to get something Tara? We'll bring it back here. What would you like Alice?"

We took his truck to go get the food. He even opened the door for me! When we got back to Alice's, we had to take the pups out first. He insisted that Alice and I eat and he'd take them out.

HEARTS BLAZING

There was no arguing with this guy. He wanted to help me in anyway he could.

As I went to bed that night at Alice's, I thought of Jonathan. But why was I thinking of him? Zack was the man I was marrying. I decided to call Zack. He gets worried when he can't get in touch with me. I reached for the phone and dialed his number. He picked up on the first ring.

"Hello?"

"Hi," I responded.

"Tara, where are you? I've been worried sick."

"I'm sorry. We got done late here at Alice's so I'm just staying here tonight."

"What? You're not at home?"

"No, I thought it best to just stay. I'll go home in the morning before coming back here for my regular shift. I'm really just too tired to drive. Alice is all I have tomorrow, since its Friday, so I could go home for awhile in the morning."

"Well I miss you. We haven't been together very much at all these past few months. Ever since that guy started doing work over there. We're getting married in two months. Have you forgotten? We still have a few things to do. I know you got your dress and we ordered the flowers and the cake. But we still have to finalize the vows for the church. Remember? Father Luke wanted us in last week and I had to cancel. Not to mention next week is Christmas and we haven't even gotten a tree yet."

"I know. I'm sorry. I'll make it up to you tomorrow. I'll leave here early. I won't stay to help Jonathan. Be over around four o'clock. We'll go get a tree and I'll fix dinner."

"Ok, that's my girl. I'll see you at four sharp tomorrow. I love you Tara, don't forget, and I miss you too."

"I know, bye."

There it was again. I didn't say I loved him. I think I'd only said it once to him throughout our entire relationship. What was I doing getting married? Well ... I knew Zack was a good guy and he was sweet. I suppose I could do worse.

The day flew by and before I knew it I was on my way home from Alice's. I told her to tell Jonathan I couldn't help him again until Monday evening. I really needed to spend the weekend with Zack. I needed to clear my head and finish our final preparations for the wedding. "I'll see you in the morning though."

"Ok honey, but I sure hope you're making the right decision."

When I pulled up to the house, Zack was already there. He jumped out of his truck and opened my door. "Hey my love." He held me in his arms and kissed me.

"Hey let a girl breathe," I laughed. I got Mya and Shadow out of the car. "I just have to feed them then we can go."

"Sounds good." Oh and I called father Luke. He said we could stop by this evening to finalize our vows, so I figure we'd go before getting the tree since it's on the way."

We went in the house and I fed the pups and looked through my mail. "Zack, before we go to see Father Luke I have to ask you something."

"Sure what is it?"

"It's about where we're going to live. I can't leave this house. I won't give up my wolves."

"First off... they're only half wolf and I've hardly seen you this past month. I was really starting to think you were having second thoughts about marrying me. I thought that you were putting your pups over me. I see how much you love them, but if that's true, I don't want to know about it. I'd rather have you and deal with your fondness for the pups, so here's what I thought. We'll live here with them and I'll rent my house out. The income could give us some extra money and you wouldn't have to work so hard. So that's my idea... what do you say?"

HEARTS BLAZING

"Zack, you're right, I was sort of having second thoughts. I do love Mya and Shadow. They're a part of me now. I know they're not full-blooded wolves, but to me they are. They're the closest I'd ever get to a real one. I've loved wolves for so long… this is like a dream to me. I know you're not a real animal lover, so you probably couldn't understand."

"I know, and I try to understand, especially how you've explained it."

"Although about my working, I'll probably work just as hard, but I might only have one job starting next week."

"Why what's going on?"

"Well, Alice and I were talking and she'd like me to start being with her all day. I was going to call Jan and see if she'd like to take over my cleaning business. I love all my customers, but Alice needs me the most. She's getting on in years and she has trouble walking lately. Plus, with that job I get to take the pups with me so they're not alone. When we get back tonight I'm going to call Jan, and if she agrees she could start in January."

"That's great! That would probably work out for the best for you and her."

"Well let's go while my babies are sleeping because they'll have to go out when we get home."

We went and talked to Father Luke and got the time we wanted for the wedding. Then we went and got a beautiful spruce tree to put up for Christmas. When we got home, Zack set the tree up in the front room while I took the pups out and started dinner. As I watched him I thought, "I do love him." It's just in my own way. It doesn't seem like a passionate love. But he's a good man.

I called Jan and explained the work situation to her.

"Oh I'd love to. I was looking for another job and this would be perfect!"

"Great! Then I'll let my customers know next week and you can

65

take over right after Christmas, which is only a couple of weeks away."

"Ok. Call me next week. Oh, how are the wedding plans coming along?"

"Good. We went and talked to Father Luke tonight so everything's all set. Did you go pick your dress up my maid of honor?" I laughed.

"Yes I did and I'll have you know it was a perfect fit." She burst into a fit of laughter.

"Ok then… till I talk to you again… goodbye," I said.

Zack stayed over night that night. It was the first time we had actually spent the night together. As I lay in bed trying to fall asleep, I thought, "Just think in another month and a half this is how every night will be with Zack." I drifted off to sleep with my mind in a state of confusion.

Chapter 13

The next morning I got up and took the pups out while I waited for my water to boil for tea. Then we left to go to Alice's. While I was there, Zack did some grocery shopping. I promised I'd only be gone for three hours.

When I got to Alice's, I told her Jan and how she was going to be taking my place on the cleaning jobs. I'd be able to start coming all day everyday for her within the next few weeks.

"Oh I'm so happy! I was hoping you'd be able to do that. You don't have to do any extra work, just keep me company," she said as she played with the pups.

"Sure, I think you just want me here for my beautiful little puppies," I laughed.

'Well that too! I love these little guys just like you do. Oh by the way, Jonathan asked about you last night. He seemed disappointed that he wasn't going to see you until Monday. In fact, when he left he said he wouldn't be back until Monday at five o'clock. Claimed he was going to rest over the weekend since he had been working so hard, but I don't really think that's what it was about. I have a feeling it was because of you."

I drove home with that thought still on my mind. When I got home, Zack was there. He had made dinner and taken the ornaments down from upstairs to decorate the tree.

"Well someone was busy today," I said as I looked at him.

67

TINA VELAZQUEZ

"Yep, I hope you don't mind. I just wanted to help you."

"No its fine," I said.

"Good. I hope it's fine too then that I moved a lot of my clothes from home into your closet. I figured that since the wedding's almost here and we've decided to live here that I should start moving in. I'll need to put most of my stuff in storage to rent the house. You really don't need anything else here."

"Yeah that's fine."

"Good! Could I stay tonight again? We could decorate the tree, maybe watch a Christmas movie and pop some popcorn?"

"Yeah that sounds good." I really didn't think I sounded convincing.

"Tomorrow neither one of us works, so maybe we could have a lazy day around here?" Zack smiled. "I haven't seen you in such a long time. I just want you all to myself," he said as he kissed me.

We feel asleep on the couch watching the Christmas movie. I woke up at around two in the morning and woke Zack. The TV was still on. "Come on into the bedroom. We feel asleep," I told him.

We both got up and went into the bedroom and fell back asleep. I don't know if it was the fact that I was really tired or I just didn't want anything to happen between us. I wondered, "What am I doing" again to myself as I drifted off to sleep.

68

Chapter 14

When the pups woke up in the morning I got up and quietly shut the door. I wanted Zack to sleep. I was going to make pancakes and surprise him.

It was after eleven o'clock when he finally woke up. "How long have you been up?" he asked in a sleepy voice.

"For a few hours. I'm an early riser even on my days off."

"Why didn't you wake me?" he asked.

"You were obviously tired and needed some extra rest. Besides, you're off today too. You don't have anything to do."

"Yeah I know. I have you all to myself today," he smiled as he came and put his arms around me.

We looked out the window together and saw it had started snowing. There was about six inches already on the ground.

It was Mya and Shadows first snow. I took them out and laughed at the way they were looking up at the sky! It was like they were wondering where the snow was coming from. They were jumping up and down almost burying themselves in it. Mya was trying to push it up with her nose. Shadow was watching her and started to do the same. We went back in the house after letting them play for a half hour. Zack had tea ready.

"Here you go. I thought you'd need something warm after all that fun out there."

"Thanks. You should have seen them. They were funny."

"I did. I watched through the window. Look at them now though."

They were curled up together fast asleep.

"I guess I wore them out," I laughed.

We watched an old classic Christmas movie that was on TV. After that, we decorated the tree and ordered a pizza for dinner. Before we knew it the day was over. It seemed like Sundays were always like that since it was my only day off.

Zack kissed me as we went to bed. "I love you, Tara." You are the best woman any man could ever want or need." He wrapped his arms tightly around me and kissed me.

"Ok," I laughed, "don't strangle me before we're even married!"

"Oh sorry! I forgot how fragile you are," he laughed.

"Hey buddy... you know there's a couch in there with your name on it."

"I don't think so. My place is right here beside my beautiful bride to be."

On that note, I fell asleep in his arms. I felt a little better, but then again I hadn't seen Jonathan in three days.

Chapter 15

On Monday morning we got up, had tea and did the routine with the pups. Zack left at about ten o'clock. "See you tonight," he said as he walked toward the door.

"Well don't forget I have to help at Alice's tonight, so if you get here before eight o'clock I probably won't be here."

"Oh that's right. Well I'll be here about eight thirty then."

The pups and I got to Alice's around noon as usual.

"Oh I missed you two!" Alice said. "And you too Tara," she laughed. The pups were jumping up and licking Alice. They were so fond of her. She really was like their grandma.

"Jonathan called said he'd be here around five o'clock. Wanted to know if you were going to be here. I told him yes. I told him you were staying until eight o'clock."

I could have sworn I saw a smile on her face.

At five o'clock on the dot Jonathan showed up at the door. I opened the door.

"Hey stranger! How was your weekend? I missed seeing you."

"Me too," I said. I told him about putting up my tree and about calling Jan to take over my cleaning jobs. I also told him about the pup's first snow, but left out whom I spent my weekend with and, of course, about seeing Father Luke.

"Where are they? Mya! Shadow!" he shouted as he came in.

They trampled over each other trying to get to him and he threw

71

himself on the floor like they knocked him down! He laughed like crazy as they jumped all over and licked his face. Alice and I started laughing too.

"They sure do like you," I said.

"Of course they do. Who wouldn't! I'm a good guy."

I stayed until eight o'clock that night and everything went fine. By the time I got home it was eight thirty and Zack was already there waiting for me. He got out of his truck when I pulled up.

"This is too long of a day for you honey. Can't you just go back to staying from noon to four o'clock?"

"No, not while her house is getting done. I have to stay to help Jonathan."

"Well what does this guy do on other jobs? He doesn't have you to help him everywhere."

"I don't know. Come on, it's cold out here."

We went in the house and I put on tea. I thought about how I really needed to get a run put up outside for Mya and Shadow. They were getting bigger and were getting harder to watch and to handle. Maybe I'd talk to Jonathan tomorrow about putting one up for me. I sat down with Zack and had our tea and some cookies I had baked that morning. Before we knew it bedtime was upon us. I was beat and fell fast asleep while Zack was still talking to me.

Chapter 16

When I woke up the next morning Zack was already gone. There was a note telling me he didn't wake me because I seemed exhausted last night. He said he'd see me tonight around eight thirty again. He hoped Alice's house was finished getting remodeled really soon.

I got up and took the pups out then, of course, made my tea. I called Jan to make sure she hadn't changed her mind about the cleaning job, since I was going to start telling everyone tomorrow. While Alice was eating her lunch, I went and put some clothes in the washer. We were going to the store while the babies slept. "Take care of the house while we are gone," I whispered to them as we walked out the door.

"I can't believe it's only a month until my wedding," I told Alice.

"As long as you're sure it's what you want. I still say you and Jonathan have some kind of connection."

"No I'm just helping him," I told her. "When he's done with your house I'll never see him again."

"Is that what you really want though? To never see him again?" she said and looked away. She seemed to hesitate before continuing. "You know I'm a pretty old lady. I've seen a thing or two in my day and I see that the two of you have a special bond. You have since the day you met. Your eyes sparkle when you see him and his do too. But if you want to be in denial, then so be it. Just remember what I've told you."

We pulled into the parking lot and I parked right in front. As we shopped, I thought about what Alice had said in the car. "What she's saying just can't be true," I thought to myself. I'm just helping him. He's a nice guy and a hard worker. I do love Zack in my own way. Just stop these thoughts!

I unpacked the groceries when we got home. I made Alice her afternoon tea and cookies. At five o'clock, as soon as the door opened, Mya and Shadow jumped up and ran to meet Jonathan.

"Ok, ok girls one at a time," he laughed. Again, he went right to the floor to play with them. I will never see Zack doing that, I thought. I started telling him about how I needed to find someone to put up a pen for me. It was getting too hard for me run after them.

"I could do it for you. In fact, I'll do it tomorrow if you want. No charge for you. I'll take the day off of my regular job. I'm ahead of schedule anyway and I have some eight-foot fencing that would work perfect."

"Oh I can't let you do it for nothing."

"No, but these guys can and it's for them not you," he laughed.

We set plans before I left that night. He would be over by nine the next morning and while I went on my cleanings he would stay with the pups and build them a pen. Then he'd meet me at Alice's in the afternoon with Mya and Shadow and we'd work until eight o'clock.

Chapter 17

The next morning, Jonathan showed up right at nine o'clock. I showed him the house.

"So this is the kitchen you hate?"

"Don't remind me," I said.

"It's not that bad, but I could fix it real nice for you if you ever decide to get it done."

"Yeah, when I win the lottery I'll give you a call," I laughed.

"We'll see, we'll see,'" he continued to say.

I went to my cleanings that day and told them all about Jan taking over the following week. Of the four of them, I'd say Martha took the news the hardest.

"Oh Tara, you've been with me for so long how will I ever cope without you?"

"That's what Jan will be here for. She'll take over where I left off. You'll like her, I promise."

"I suppose, but I'll miss you. You brighten my day when you come here."

"You won't miss me because I'm going to stay in touch with you."

"Oh please do that, would you? It would be so nice to still see you every once in a while."

Millie, Mary and Jill all said about the same thing, that they would miss me. But they all understood that Alice needed me more. I told them Jan would be good for them and they'd like her. They all wished me good luck and said not to forget about them. I got to Alice's right at noon.

"Where are my babies?" she wanted to know.

"Well, Jonathan will be bringing them."

"Jonathan? Well, well... what's going on? Do tell."

"Nothing like what you're thinking! Remember? He was putting up the run for them today."

"Oh yeah, this old lady forgot. Well how did your ladies take the news today about your friend taking over the cleanings?"

"Pretty good actually. I think Martha took it the hardest, but I promised to keep in touch with all of them."

The doorbell rang. It was June. "Hey what are you doing here?" I asked.

"Well I came to see you of course," she came in laughing. "Hi Alice."

"June, what a pleasant surprise."

"I was on my way to the store, so I thought I'd stop to see you."

"I'm glad you're here," Tara said. I went on to tell June about Jan taking over.

"Oh I'm going to miss your cleaning Tara. She better be as good as you! I won't miss you too much because I could always come here to see you."

"Hey, I just thought of a great idea!" I told them.

"What's that?" Alice asked.

"Well, so no one misses me and I don't miss anyone, why don't we start up a little senior club that could meet here once a week? I could fix a light lunch and everyone could take turns bringing sweets. You could all get to know each other and play cards or something."

Alice's face lit up. "That would be wonderful. We could even do this in my basement that hasn't seen a party in years! And the sweets sound like the best part!"

"I should have known you'd say that, miss sweet tooth."

HEARTS BLAZING

"When can we start?" June asked.

"First things first, my dear. Maybe right after I get married."

Just then Jonathan walked in.

"Oh my, who we have here?" June asked.

Alice explained who he was. He had Mya and Shadow with him. They ran right up to me.

"These must be the hybrids you told me about," June said.

"Yes they are."

"They are beautiful just like you said."

I introduced June to the pups. She adored them just like everyone else did. Except for Zack, of course.

"Wait until you get home and see the run Tara. You're going to love it. I even put some plastic on top so if it rains they won't get wet. I put it down two of the sides too," he said as he winked at me. "Oh here, I almost forgot, I picked up a shake for you on the way over. I knew you had a lot of work today and didn't think you'd have time to eat."

"Thank you Zack. That's so thoughtful of you. You're right too. I had to tell everyone today about it being my last week with them, so I was at everyone's house a little longer today."

"No problem. Anything for you little lady. Well drink up. I'm going to start sanding in the bedroom," he smiled.

He brushed the top of my head as he walked by. When he was gone, I noticed June give Alice a knowing look.

"Don't take this the wrong way, but I think that man has a crush on you," June said.

"Oh come on... you too?"

"What do you mean?"

"Well I told her the same thing," Alice said. "Ever since they've met she's seemed more happy and she's always singing to herself."

"Oh you two don't know what you're talking about."

"We'll see," June said.

77

TINA VELAZQUEZ

June was getting ready to leave and they both talked excitedly about how they would see each other more often now that I was going to get this little senior club going. I had never seen Alice so happy. Well, except when she was with Mya and Shadow. It felt good. I wouldn't miss my ladies and they could all become friends. It will be really nice.

Chapter 18

The next few weeks flew by. Before I knew it, the wedding was a week away. I had everything set up with my ladies to meet at Alice's on Mondays at one o'clock in the afternoon. They would play cards or bunko. I was even going to get a bingo game! They would take turns bringing a desert and Alice would provide the light lunch of sandwiches and tea. They all told me Jan was doing a good job and although she wasn't me, they were happy with her.

Jonathan was almost done with Alice's house. He still didn't know that I was getting married. A few days before the wedding, he told me that he hated the fact he was almost done with Alice's house. He said that he'd never had so much fun on a job and he was really going to miss me. He wanted me to talk Alice into getting more work done.

"I have to tell you the truth," he said as he looked into my eyes. We were standing in her kitchen. "I could have been done here weeks ago, but I couldn't stand the thought of not seeing you anymore. Mya and Shadow too. I've really come to love you. Them I mean," he seemed to flush.

"Oh my!" I thought. Were Alice and June right? I felt like I was going to cry. Deep down I knew I was going to miss him too. At that moment it felt like someone was ripping my heart right out of my chest. What does this mean? Why am I feeling this? I couldn't talk. I was afraid if I opened my mouth nothing would come out. Besides,

I had no idea what to say anyway. I just looked at him as tears welled up in my eyes. I think that was the moment I knew I loved him. I would miss him. I couldn't imagine my life without him, without seeing him everyday, without being near him, talking to him and helping him.

Then it happened. He took me in his arms and very lightly kissed my lips. I felt a tear and wondered if it was his or mine. When he pulled away I realized the tears on my face were coming from my own eyes. We stood there looking at each other.

"Go out to dinner with me Tara," he said.

As if I didn't know where the words were coming from, I heard myself say ok. What was I thinking? But I had to. If I didn't go I'd never know for sure. I'd never know what I was missing.

We went out to dinner and just talked about everything. He kissed me again when he dropped me off. I went into the house wondering what was going on. I was getting married the day after tomorrow... what was I doing with this man?

"I'll see you tomorrow, right?" he asked.

"Sure, tomorrow we'll meet again," I said.

The pups were jumping all around when I got in the house. My answering machine was flashing. It was Zack wishing me a goodnight and telling me he was excited that it was only a day until the wedding. I felt guilty. What was I going to do?

I had to think. One more day and I'd have to forget about Jonathan. I was getting married. I'd have to forget how he held me in his arms, about how his lips caressed mine. How was I going to do that? Did I even want to forget? "I had to forget," I thought. I just had too.

I went to bed and had a very restless night. I couldn't stop thinking about Jonathan. Zack had never been on my mind like this. Oh, what did I get myself into? I finally drifted off to sleep, only to dream of Jonathan. We were on a secluded beach. There was a huge blanket spread out and we were lying on top of it. He was telling me he loved

HEARTS BLAZING

me deeply and couldn't live without me. I was telling him the same. When he kissed me, his lips were soft and warm and wet. His tongue entered my mouth as if exploring. I felt his hands caressing my body and heard him saying my name over and over...

Then the pups started howling. I woke with a start, remembering the dream. What was going on? I rolled out of bed. I have Helen and June's to clean today. This was my last time cleaning for them before Jan took over. Zack wouldn't be over again tonight because I told him I had to do a lot of work at Alice's before the wedding. I started wondering if that was just an excuse for me to see as much of Jonathan as I could. I headed over to Helen's. I told her about Jan taking over for me and about the little senior club I was starting.

"Oh that will be so much fun for us old timers!" She was so excited. I don't think I had ever seen her like that. "I'll get to see you every Monday then, even though you won't be cleaning anymore," she said. Do you want me to bring the dessert next week? I could make a chocolate cake, since you said Alice likes chocolate so much?"

"That would be great," I told her. "We'll have to make up some sort of chart so we know whose turn it is to bring something."

"Oh I can hardly wait until Monday! This was such a wonderful idea you had. I think you're in the wrong business," she said.

"I don't know about that. I think I'm right where I belong."

"Oh I just remembered! Tomorrow's the big day for you! Are you ready?"

"As ready as I'll ever be," I replied, sounding not so convincing.

"You don't seem too thrilled about this Tara. Are you sure you're doing the right thing?"

"Of course," I mumbled.

As I went about cleaning I realized that I wasn't sure if I was doing the right thing. So why am I doing it? I left Helen's with a smile and hug from her.

TINA VELAZQUEZ

"I'll see you tomorrow at your wedding, my dear."

I got to June's and I told her how Helen was going to be the first to bring desert next week.

"Good. I'll take the following week if that's ok."

"Sure is! I have to make some sort of chart so we'll know whose turn it is every week."

"Yeah, that would be good. So are you ready for your big day tomorrow?" she asked.

"Tomorrow at this time I'll be a wife. Can you believe it?"

"Tara, I don't mean to intrude, but you don't seem all that happy for someone who's getting married tomorrow. Now I know it's none of my business, but I've seen the way you and Jonathan look at each other. Are you really sure about tomorrow?"

"Sure I am. I know this thing happened fast, but I'm not getting any younger you know," I laughed.

"I know sweetheart, but to be happy you need to have a man that loves you deeply. A man that you love deeply in return. Life is too short to just settle. Do you know what I mean?"

I have no idea why, but all of a sudden I started pouring my heart out to June. I told her how I went out to dinner with Jonathan and how I felt butterflies when he kissed me. Something I never felt with Zack. But Zack loved me and treated me good. I was so confused.

"Follow your heart Tara. It's not too late. Don't ever think it's too late."

Before I could respond, I realized it was time for me to pick up Mya and Shadow and go to Alice's. And then when I got there, I knew I had to make the final calls for tomorrow. To make sure the flowers and cake would be where they were supposed to be and at the right time. As I was doing all this, I felt like I was just going through the motions. I realized I didn't seem happy at all. Not until Jonathan walked in the door. When he smiled at me and said "Hey," my heart melted. My eyes began to well up with tears as I realized that this, this man standing in my doorway, this was the man I love. I mean, really love.

82

HEARTS BLAZING

That night, when we got done working, it was a little after eight o'clock. He asked me to go with him to his house. "You can bring the pups. I just need to talk to you."

He seemed so serious and sincere that I couldn't say no. We got to his house and took Mya and Shadow out of the car. "I'll put them in the back. I have a place they can go." He let me in the front door. When he came back in, he asked if I wanted something to drink. "Tea would be nice," I said.

"Ok then go sit down and I'll get us some."

I was looking around his front room as he went into the kitchen. He had a nice house. A little plain, but nice.

"Do you to watch TV or listen to the radio?" he asked

"Whatever you want. It doesn't matter to me," I replied.

I don't think I had ever been so nervous in my life. I wondered what he had to talk to me about. He decided to put on the radio. It was some nice slow music. He got up from the couch and held out his hand.

"Dance with me. Let me hold you close to me."

I got up as if in a trance. Oh what was I doing? But I couldn't help it. I wanted to be here. I needed to be here. We danced to a few songs then he said, "I really need to talk to you."

He sounded so serious. He put me on the couch and sat facing me. Then he got up, rubbed his hands together nervously, and kneeled on the floor in front of me. "Tara, a few days ago Alice told me your getting married tomorrow. is this true?"

"Yes it is," I whispered. I could barely hear myself.

"I have to ask you what you'll probably think is a stupid question, but do you love this guy?"

"I don't know anymore," I said

"Did you ever love him? Did you love him before we kissed last night?"

"I don't know. After kissing you last night, I'm very confused. I

83

love him in some ways, but I'm beginning to think I'm not in love with him. There's a difference. It's almost like you can love someone, but not like who they are."

"Tara, let me ask you something. Did you feel anything when I kissed you?"

"Yes Jonathan. I felt alive. I felt butterflies. I went to sleep and had a dream about you. You're all I've been thinking of. I just didn't want to admit it to myself. I don't want to hurt Zack. He's really a nice guy, but what I feel for you is different. It's stronger. I don't know how to explain it."

"Let me ask you this. Can you see yourself never seeing me again? Because you know, after what happened last night, I won't be able to see you again once your married. It will be too hard for me to not want to pull you in my arms and kiss you, to protect you and to love you. Yes Tara, to love you. I love you Tara."

"Oh!" was all that came out of my mouth. I couldn't even think of an answer.

"Don't do it Tara, don't marry this guy. Not yet at least. Give me a chance to show you how much I love you and how I can make you happy. I know I could.

"Jonathan, I don't know what to say. Everything is set for tomorrow. How can I cancel now?"

"Tara, come with me." He got up from the floor and took my hand. I followed him. I didn't know how to stop it. It was as if I were in some kind of a trance. We went into the bedroom. He sat me on the bed and then lit three candles next to me on the dresser. He unbuttoned his shirt and dropped it to the floor. Kneeling down, he slowly slipped off my shoes. I was speechless. This man was remarkable. I could never envision this happening with Zack. He reached toward me again and raised my shirt over my head, taking his time and gazing into my eyes. As he started to unfasten my bra, he titled his head and caressed my lips with his. "Tara, give me the

HEARTS BLAZING

chance to show you I could love you the way you deserve to be loved. Let me make love to you."

"Oh Jonathan," was all I could say. I felt like I was in a dream. My body was aching for him. Wanting to be in his arms and wanting to kiss him. He finished taking off my clothes and laid me down on the bed. Then he took off his own shoes and pants and lay down next to me.

"You're beautiful in every way," he said. He kissed my eyes, my cheeks and my lips and then moved on to places that I had never been kissed before. He looked up at me and said, "Tara, I haven't been with a woman in more than three years. I haven't even desired to until you came along. Please tell me if I'm doing anything to hurt you. I would never want to do anything like that."

"You're not hurting me at all Jonathan. You're making me feel very loved. Possibly the most love I've ever felt before."

"Tara, I love you. Marry me. Don't marry him. You don't love him. I know you love me. Don't leave…don't make me lose this feeling I have with you." As he kissed me, I felt tears drop onto my face.

"I do love you Jonathan. I love you too."

He looked at me and smiled. I had never in my life been made love to the way Jonathan made love to me that night. I must have drifted off for a few minutes because the next thing I knew he was walking back into the bedroom with Mya and Shadow alongside. They jumped on the bed and he laughed and jumped on the bed with them.

"Guess what you two! She loves me! We're going to be a family! She loves me and I love her and we both love you girls more than anything," he laughed.

When I woke in the morning, we were all still on the bed. Jonathan had his arm around Shadow and Mya was lying across our feet.

"Come on girls," I said quietly, trying not to wake Jonathan. I got dressed and took Mya and Shadow out of the room. I peeked back

85

in at Jonathan and smiled with tears in my eyes, then went in and kissed him on the head. "I love you, I do. You are my true love. I love you in every way a woman can love a man. Everything about you. I'll never forget you. I'll go to my grave with you on my mind. With this night engraved with your name in my heart. I love you Jonathan."

I turned and walked out the door with my pups, my heart shattering in a million pieces.

Chapter 19

When we got home, I noticed Zack had called six times just that morning. Every message was the same. He loved me, he couldn't wait for me to be his wife and he could even tolerate the pups for me. And he couldn't wait to see me at the church.

He could tolerate the pups? What was that? Jonathan loves them just as much as I do. He wasn't just tolerating them. I was finally seeing one of the major differences between him and Jonathan. How was I ever going to go through with this? I didn't want to hurt Zack, but was a willing to marry him at my expense? Marriage was supposed to be for life. How could I marry Zack knowing it was Jonathan that I loved?

It was time for me to get ready to go to the church. To go through with this commitment I had made to Zack. Jan was meeting me at the church, so I started getting dressed myself. I didn't know how I would get my makeup done, I couldn't stop my crying and my mascara kept running down my cheeks. I can't do this. I want to go back to Jonathan. Oh please give me the strength to get through this. What was I doing? My happiness lay with a handyman, a lover of dogs and a good man. Happiness did not wait at the church where I was getting ready to go.

When I arrived, Jan was waiting at the door. "You're a little late, don't you think? Wow, you look like hell! What's wrong?" she asked.

I told her all about Jonathan. "What am I going to do? I can't picture my life without him. I can't see myself with Zack any longer, even though he loves me and he's good to me. How can I not do this and hurt him? I made a commitment to him. What should I do Jan?" I cried.

"Tara, all I can say is marriage is supposed to be for life. You need to follow your heart. Whatever you decide, I'm here for you."

She was the second person who told me to follow my heart in the past two days. I looked out into the church…

It was supposed to be the happiest day of a woman's life. The church blossomed with beautiful, colorful flowers. The bridesmaids lingered in their baby blue dresses; the groomsmen in their black tuxes. Friends and relatives all so excited for the young couple filled the church. The groom stood in anticipation at the altar for his beautiful bride. I could picture all this clearly as I waited in the back room with my maid of honor and best friend, Jan. My mind raced, knowing that soon I would walk down the aisle. Thinking that, in a few minutes, I would lay eyes upon my eager, soon-to-be husband. Wondering how I was going to be able to go through with this after what happened last night.

It just happened. It wasn't planned. What is planned is this wedding. Planned down to the very last little detail. I know everyone is out there waiting for me to make my entrance into my new life. I know I have to go through with this. I can't disappoint the man who had come to love me so much over the months that he was willing to go to any length for me. He adored and worshiped me. I just had to do this…didn't I?

The image of last night burned in my mind. The arms of another man. The passion that was never there with Zack. I had to somehow forget it. But how? How could I forget those deep feelings, the feelings of real love that I only have for Jonathan?

Just go, I told myself, and do what you have made a commitment to do…

HEARTS BLAZING

Just then the back door to the church burst open.

"Tara!" Jonathan yelled, trying to catch his breath.

"Jonathan!!" I exclaimed in return. I was shocked to see him there.

Jan walked out of the back room and looked back and forth between me and Jonathan. "You must be Jonathan," she said.

"Yeah, I am."

"She loves you. Don't let her do this. It's not what she really wants. You're the one she wants."

"I know. I heard her this morning before she left. I just didn't know what to do at the time. Then decided if I didn't stop this craziness I'd lose her forever. And I'm not about to let that happen," he smiled at Tara.

Jan looked over and smiled at Tara "You're my best friend Tara. I don't want to see you make a mistake. You need to follow your heart. I'm with you all the way."

I hugged her tight, saying thank you.

"Go on now you two. Just go and I'll take care of everything else. I'll go explain that there isn't going to be a wedding."

"How are you going to do that?" Tara asked.

"Don't worry about it. Just go with Jonathan. Call me later."

Jonathan and I went out the back door of the church and climbed together into his truck. We drove to my house first and picked up Mya and Shadow, then went back to his house. When we got there, I went straight to the bedroom to change out of my wedding dress, putting on some clothes we grabbed when we stopped at my house. When I went back out to the front room, he had tea and cookies waiting for me.

"Tara, it'll be ok. I love you," Jonathan whispered in my ear.

"I love you too," I said.

I suddenly realized I never said that to Zack, never meant it at least. Oh how he must feel right now. I couldn't even imagine. What did Jan tell everyone? What did she tell Zack? Oh what a mess I made.

Jonathan must have seen the distress on my face because he said, "Don't worry baby I'm here for you. I'll be here when you call him. I'll be your strength. You did the right thing. You'd feel much worse now if you would have went through with it. Tara you've been my best friend, and now my lover, and soon you will be my wife. That's the way it should be. That's the way it was meant to be. Don't worry, your beautiful wedding dress won't go to waste," he laughed.

I laughed too. He kissed me and I felt him tremble. I knew I had done the right thing. There was not a doubt in my mind.

"Oh, here... I almost forgot," Jonathan said.

"What's this?"

"Well it is Valentine's Day, isn't it?"

He handed me a card and a big box of candy with a little red and white bear that said "I LOVE YOU."

"Oh Jonathan." I had never felt so touched.

"Thank you. This makes me feel much better."

"Come here," he said. He took me in his arms and kissed me. ""Come on, there's got to be a good love story on TV for us to watch. You know Tara, there will never be a love story as good as our own," he winked.

I gave him a big kiss and said, "I am so glad you did what you did today, showing up at the church. I wouldn't have been able to stay with him. You would have always been on my mind. Thank you."

"You're welcome. Tara, I will love you for the rest of my life. You will never regret choosing me."

He kissed me and hugged me so tight I thought I wouldn't be able to breathe. We both laughed.

"Before settling in for the night, I think I have a few calls I better make."

Zack was very understanding. "I know you do. Do you want me to give you some privacy?"

"No. I have nothing to hide from you. If we are going to have a good relationship, we better have trust in each other and not hide things. Otherwise, there'd be no relationship," Tara said.

I called Jan first. She told me what happened at the church. She told Father Luke there wasn't going to be a wedding. Then she talked to Zack and told him that it was just too fast for me to get married. She said Zack stood up and told everyone that something had come up, according to his fiancé's friend, and that the wedding was not going to take place that day.

She said there was a few mumbles from the pews, but everyone left the church pretty quickly. When she got outside, all the little ladies that I cleaned for called her over and asked what happened. Then Jan started laughing.

"What?" I asked.

"You should have seen them all looking at me with raised eyebrows and confused expressions on their faces. I almost started cracking up. That Alice lady was like, 'Come on Jan, tell us what really happened! It had to do with Jonathan, right?' Then June said, 'Yeah, remember the way they were looking at each other at your house?' Jan was laughing again. They're really all very funny. Anyway, I told them they'd have to ask you on Monday. I didn't know if you wanted me to tell them."

"Oh Jan, thank you. I don't know how to thank you enough."

"Don't worry. Just rest tonight. Let Jonathan take care of you. You made the right choice. I noticed the way the two of you looked at each other."

"Thanks again Jan." I said my good-bye.

Chapter 20

It was Friday and I didn't have to go to Alice's until Monday. She was giving me Saturday off, so I had three days to spend with Jonathan. I dialed Zack's number.

"Here goes," I told Jonathan. He squeezed my hand.

"Hello," he answered on the first ring. He sounded like he had been crying. I felt terrible at that moment.

"Zack, it's me Tara."

"Tara, are you ok? What happened? How could you do that to me? It was supposed to be our big day."

I know Zack. I'm sorry, but everything just moved so fast. I was confused."

"Well I'll be over soon and we'll talk. We'll set a different date. Everything will be ok."

I knew it was better for me to just make a clean break and not prolong it with Zack.

"No Zack, that wouldn't be a good idea."

"What do you mean? We need to see each other."

"No Zack. I'm not even home. I…. There isn't going to be another date set." ?

"What do you mean? Of course we can set another date. Oh Tara, there someone else isn't there? It's that guy that you've been spending all you're evenings with at that lady's house, isn't it?"

I couldn't lie. I wasn't a liar. "Yes Zack it is. I'm sorry. I didn't mean for it to happen. It just did."

92

HEARTS BLAZING

"I see," was all he said.

"So what do we do now then Tara? I guess I should come by next week and get my things. I haven't moved my furniture into storage yet, thank goodness for that. I did have someone lined up to rent the house. I'm hurt Tara. I'm really hurt."

"I know. I'm so sorry. I don't know what else to say. I'm not this kind of person. I don't really know how this happened."

"Well I'll get my things next week. I'll call first. Take care Tara, and tell this guy he's one lucky person." I heard the phone click.

"I feel like a horrible person," I told Jonathan.

"You're not, you're a lady who has now found true love. Let me draw you a nice warm bubble bath. When you get out we'll watch a movie and have tea."

"Alright, maybe it would help," I said.

We did exactly what he said and then we went to bed. He just held me in his arms and kept telling me how much he loved me. We were going to have a wonderful life together.

"Maybe we could even work together. You were such a good helper," he said.

93

Chapter 21

In the morning we got up and made coffee together. We lounged around all morning watching cartoons, something I hadn't done in years. Jonathan wouldn't even let me get dressed. He said this was going to be my lazy weekend.

That night, we ordered out dinner and just snuggled on the couch watching TV. He just kept kissing me and telling me how happy he was to have met me and how happy we were going to be for the rest of our lives.

Chapter 22

On Sunday morning we woke and took out Mya and shadow. I watched as Jonathan played with them. I never thought I would have found a man so sweet and caring. After we had some pancakes for breakfast, we decided to go see Alice.

"Won't she be surprised," Jonathan said.

"Well I don't know about surprised," I replied.

"Why, what do you mean?" he asked.

I went on to tell him about what she had said to me. Then about what her and June had said to Jan.

He was laughing.

"What's so funny?" I asked.

"Well I guess you were the only one that didn't know we were falling in love. I know Alice knew and apparently so did June. Every night when I saw you Tara, I fell more in love with you. Every night as we worked side by side, I couldn't picture my life without you. You were the only blind one. But you know what's good?"

"What?" I asked.

"That I won out in the end. That you are mine and I'm never letting you get away." He took me in his arms and kissed me. "I love you Tara."

"I love you Jonathan."

We got over to Alice's around noon with Mya and Shadow in tow.

"Well, well," she said as we walked in the door. "I knew it. I knew it all along. Look at the two smiling faces that just walked through my door. Sit down, the both of you, and tell me the story." Alice listened most attentively. She had this huge smile on her face as she kept petting the pups. "So what happens now?" she asked.

"Well, this wonderful woman is going to be my wife. And the sooner the better," Jonathan said, smiling.

"Oh, however can we do that? I was just supposed to get married to someone else! I can't plan a big wedding again," I said.

"Ok, so we'll have a small one. We'll just go get married in the church and then have a small get together with friends. With just all your ladies you worked for," Jonathan said.

"Oh that would be nice. How about if you use the downstairs room? It hasn't seen a party in years. We used to celebrate every holiday, birthday and anniversary in there when my husband was alive. When he died, a huge part of me died with him. Even though he's still here in my heart, I miss his touch. I miss being able to see his face and hear his voice. Don't waste another day without each other. Life is too precious and too short.

When Alice finished talking, I saw she had a far away look in her eyes. Almost like she was with her husband again. I felt sorry for her. I could tell that she loved him dearly and I knew it must be really hard for her to live without him.

"You could have all the friends in the world, but your spouse is the one you're closest to. No other can feel that special bond."

I looked at Jonathan and saw he was looking at me.

"Well?" he asked.

"Ok, I'm convinced! Whatever you want is ok with me," Tara said.

We left Alice's and told her we would both be there tomorrow around noon. We were going to finish up the painting. Jonathan was taking off of work again because he was ahead of schedule. We got

HEARTS BLAZING

back to Jonathan's and made some sandwiches for lunch. We watched the news together and played with Mya and Shadow.

"Ok, so tomorrow when we're at Alice's, I want you to call Father Luke. Explain everything to him and see what date you can get for our wedding. The sooner the better, right? I don't want to spend a day without you," he said.

"Well, where will we live? We haven't even talked about that."

"We could stay here or we could stay at your house. Whatever you want is fine with me."

"I like it here, but my house has been in the family for so long, I really hate to leave it."

"Ok then, it's settled. We'll move into your house," he said.

"If you'll let me, I'll move in tomorrow after we're done at Alice's. We could start packing tonight if you want to help me. In fact, I'll make a deal with you. If you help me pack tonight and move in tomorrow, on Tuesday night I'll start remodeling your kitchen. Anyway you want, anything you want."

"I can't let you do all that! I don't have the money."

He held up his hand. "Who said anything about money? I'll do it. I'll take care of it. You'd be helping me too, you know. In fact, if it'll make you feel any better, it could be your wedding gift from me to you. Deal?" he asked.

"Deal!" I said, kissing him."

97

Chapter 23

The next day, we got to Alice's and finished up the work. I made her dinner and we stayed and ate with her. I could tell she was so happy. "We had fun today," she commented.

"Yeah we did," I replied. I had forgotten that The Senior Club was going to take place that day, and of course I got drilled by all of the ladies about what happened at the wedding.

When they met Jonathan though, they all understood why. They all thought I had made the right decision and were happy for me. They all said the same thing. They could see the love we had for each other in our eyes. In the way we looked at each other. That night when we got home, I called Jan and told her what was going on with the new wedding. She was excited.

"Ok, so do I still get to be the maid of honor and wear the dress?" she laughed.

"Yeah, but its going to be very small. Just all the ladies that I've cleaned for. Alice, the one that I'm with everyday, said we could have a party in her basement and she wants to pay for the catering, so I guess that's what we'll do!"

I told her I had talked to Father Luke and he had an opening in a few weeks on a Saturday, so that's when we'd do it. We hung up and I told Jonathan, "You know, I'm going to have to call Zack. He has to get his clothes out of here."

"Well, I'm going to be leaving right now to pack some of my stuff

98

HEARTS BLAZING

to bring over, so why don't you call him and see when he can come?"

"That sounds good, but let me call him before you leave."

I called Zack and he said he'd be over in about an hour. I told him I'd pack up for him since it was only clothes.

"I feel kind of bad," I told Jonathan. But what was I supposed to do? I don't think I ever loved him not the way I love Jonathan. I made the right decision. I knew I did.

The pick up of his clothes went smoothly. He wanted me to be happy and wished me luck. He said in a way he could see I wasn't really into being his wife, but he loved me and didn't care.

"It's better you did this now than after we were married, Tara. You would have probably left me years down the road when you figured it out. I have to thank you for that, because it would have been harder later."

He left and when I shut the door I looked to Mya and Shadow. "It would have never worked. He didn't even say goodbye to you two."

I sat down to wait for Jonathan. He showed up an hour later.

"Let me help you unload," I said when he arrived.

"No, you stay here," he said.

"I will not! I can't sit and not help you! Especially when you're going to be doing all that work in the kitchen."

"I told you that's a wedding gift."

"Oh come on," I said stubbornly, putting my hands on my hips. He did the same. "I tell you what. This is how you can help me. I'll put these boxes in the bedroom and you sit your sweet little fanny in there and put the clothes away where you want them to go. How's that? It'll be your first wifely job," he laughed.

"My what?" I laughed.

"Please," he was putting his lip out and pouting, so I just caved in and agreed.

Chapter 24

The next morning he left for work at eight. I didn't have to be at Alice's until ten o'clock. I was on my new schedule now of Monday to Saturday ten a.m. until three p.m. Jonathan loved it. He said I needed a rest. He would rather I went to work with him, but I told him I couldn't leave Alice. He understood, but he said when I no longer had that job I could choose between staying home or helping him. I had laughed at him in response, saying," Oh... really?"

That night he came home and started work in the kitchen. He said he would spend all week just tearing things out and on Sunday we'd go pick out all new stuff. I was really happy and excited. I couldn't believe this kitchen was finally getting done after all these years.

We went to bed that night and Jonathan made such sweet love to me again. I couldn't believe my lucky fortune. So this is what real love feels like. This is passionate love. He kissed me tenderly as I rubbed the back of his head.

"I love you," he whispered.

"I love you too," I said.

We fell asleep in each other's arms. I had never felt so loved, so alive or so happy. This is going to be the rest of my life.

Chapter 25

Sunday came very quickly. We went to the store and ordered everything we were going to need for our new kitchen. We picked up food on the way home and decided to watch a movie before going to bed. We talked about our wedding that was only six days away. We had already ordered the food and cake. The church was all set. The ladies were going to decorate the basement at Alice's on Monday when The Senior Club met. Everything was under control and planned out. This was definitely going to happen.

On Monday morning, I baked a cake before going to Alice's. I knew the ladies would be busy decorating, so I told them I would bring dessert for them. I got to Alice's around ten o'clock that day and June was already there. So was Mary. She had come with June.

"Hello ladies," I said as I came into the front room.

"Hello," they all replied.

By one o'clock everyone else was there. Martha, Millie and Jill came together. Then Helen arrived last. Everyone was talking at once. They were all so excited. June went in the other room and came out with a handful of presents.

"What's all that?' I asked.

"These are all for you and Jonathan," she said. "They're sort of a pre-wedding presents from all of us because we love you so much. Tara, we're all so happy for you. That you finally have a happy heart."

101

"Oh you guys are too much!"

"Come on, open them! I can't wait to see your eyes," Alice said. I started opening the gifts and couldn't believe my eyes. Everything was wolf-themed! There was a creamer and sugar bowl. A salt-and-pepper shaker. A six-piece plate setting, a wolf canister set and two little wolf statues that had "Mya" and "Shadow" engraved on them.

"I don't know what to say!" I cried, tears welling in my eyes.

"You guys are so great! You didn't have to do this!"

"We know we didn't have to," Alice replied. "We wanted too. After all, look at all you and Jonathan did for me and what you're doing for me still," Alice said.

"Yeah and how about us?" Martha asked. "What would we have done without you all of these years?"

"Yeah and even getting us a replacement for you when you started staying with Alice," Helen added.

"We all hated to see you go, but then look what you did! You started The Senior Club for us. We made some really good new friends and we still get to be in your life," Mary said.

"Yeah! And hopefully she'll give us all the juicy details of her new life with that gorgeous man she's marrying!" Millie chimed in.

"Thank you! Thank you so much from Jonathan and myself. We'll have a wolf-themed kitchen. I'm even going to put up some wolf border on the walls to go with everything."

I went and made their light lunch and brought out the cake I had baked for them while they went downstairs to decorate. They had decided they wouldn't play cards today since we'd be setting up for the wedding.

When Jonathan got home that night, of course, he greeted Mya and Shadow first. Then he came up to me with a single red rose. "For my wife to be." He tenderly kissed my lips. "What smells so good?" he asked.

HEARTS BLAZING

"I have chicken in the oven. It's almost done. Just wait until you see what the ladies gave us today."

"Bring it on honey. Let me see."

I showed him all the kitchen things and he agreed that it all was beautiful. He said the wallpaper border would be nice in the kitchen and everything would work out just fine. We ate dinner and before you knew it, it was time for bed. We were both so tired we immediately fell asleep.

Chapter 26

Tuesday morning I went to the store before going over to Alice's. I knew I would be taking Alice later, but I'd probably be at her house longer than my frozen food would allow. After I got home and put the groceries away, I took Mya and Shadow outside for a little while. They were getting big. Probably fifty pounds by now. I watched as they jumped over each other and rolled on top of one another. They were turning out to be very beautiful. Mya was all white with blue eyes and Shadow was white underneath, but had a lot of gray on top with blue eyes. Shadow was still the shy one, always seeming to stay behind her sister. As I put them in the car, they started to get really excited. They knew by now that everyday they were going to Alice's to play. And, just like always, as soon as we got there, she gave them treats and petted them.

When we got back home that night, I don't know who was spoiling them worse! I was so happy to have found a man who loved them as much as I did. I can honestly say now that Zack didn't even like them.

"Hey baby how was your day," Jonathan asked as he put his arms around me and gave me a kiss.

"Good. I took Alice to the beauty shop and to the store. She's all excited about Saturday!"

"She's not the only one excited," he said. "Just think… you'll be legally mine. You'll have to obey me then," he laughed.

HEARTS BLAZING

"Uh… I don't think they say that anymore," I laughed back. "We'll see," he snickered. "How about going with me tonight to get a suit. I don't want to wait until the last minute."

"Sure. Where do you want to go?"

He named a store that wasn't too far from the house. So after dinner, we went and found him a suit for the wedding. By the time we got back home, it was already late. I made us some tea while he took our babies out. When we went to bed that night, he held me in his arms and kissed me.

"I am such a lucky man… and you are such a lucky woman!" he said jokingly as he tried to tickle me. "Oh… you're not ticklish," he said as he tried again.

"No, but you are," I said to him as I tickled him in return.

"Stop… stop!" he begged. "You're too much for me!" Then he reached out for my face, caressing me with his hands as he said, "With all my heart and soul, Tara, I love you, and I will take care of you and cherish you until the day I die." He was on the verge of tears.

"I love you too, Jonathan. I also will love, cherish and take care of you until the day I die."

We kissed deeply and made love.

Chapter 27

The rest of the week flew by and before I knew it, it was already Friday night. Jonathan and I were at Alice's. I had cooked dinner over there, so he was meeting me there when he was done working. We wanted to make sure everything was set for tomorrow.

"Looks good," we all said at the same time.

"Ok, where to go from here?" Jonathan asked.

"We have to stop off to see Father Luke really quick and then just home!"

We bid goodnight to Alice and told her we'd see her at three o'clock tomorrow at the church. June would be picking her up.

"Goodnight my dears. Sleep tight and don't be nervous."

We left to see Father Luke. He just wanted to make sure everything was ok for tomorrow.

"Yes, we'll be here by two forty-five," I told him.

Chapter 28

We spent the following morning being lazy. We watched cartoons. I made pancakes for breakfast and we played with the pups. Then I called Jan.

"Now don't forget! Don't be late," I told her.

"Have I ever been late?" she laughed.

"No... so don't make this a first time."

Jonathan started getting ready at one o'clock. "Come on. Shouldn't you be getting dressed?" he asked.

"We have two more hours," I told him.

"I know, but I don't want to be late. We should get there early. Maybe by two thirty," he said.

I started laughing. "Don't worry, I'm not backing out."

"I'm not worried. I just want to be prepared," he said.

I just looked at him. He looked so handsome. I don't think I'd ever seen anyone so handsome or so happy. Seeing him this way made me happy.

We arrived at the church at two forty. Some of the ladies were already there.

Then it was finally time for the ceremony.

"Christ calls you into union with him and one another. I ask you now in the presence of God and this congregation to declare your intent. Will you have this man to be your husband, to live together in a Holy marriage? Will you love him, comfort him, honor and keep him in sickness and in health, and forsaking all others, be faithful to him as long as you both shall live?" he asked.

"I will," I replied.

Then he went on to say to Jonathan, "Will you have this woman to be your wife, to live together in a holy marriage? Will you love her, honor her and keep her in sickness and in health, and forsaking all others, be faithful to her as long as you both shall live?"

"I will," Jonathan answered.

As we had said our vows, I felt tears well up in my eyes. I was so happy. I couldn't believe this was actually taking place. As Jonathan said his vows to me, I noticed he too had tears in his eyes. Before you knew it, Father Luke was announcing us as husband and wife. I heard him say the words "You may now kiss the bride," as Jonathan gently leaned in for the most beautiful kiss I had ever experienced. Everyone clapped for us.

The party afterwards at Alice's was beautiful. We had good food, a spectacular cake, music and of course more gifts. Most of the ladies got up and danced and laughed and just had a good time. When the night was over, everyone left telling us what a good time they had and wished us the best.

"You are the perfect couple," June said. "I told you to follow your heart," she whispered to me.

Jonathan surprised me when we pulled up in front of the house. He told me to wait in the truck. A few minutes later, he came out with a bag. Mya and Shadow were still in the truck with me since they had been at the church and the party. He got back in the truck and said, "Ok we're ready!"

"Ready for what? Are we going somewhere?"

"Well you didn't think we were staying here for our wedding night, did you?"

"I guess I never really thought about it."

"We're just going right down the road some until Monday."

HEARTS BLAZING

"What about Mya and Shadow?" I asked.

"They're going with us. You didn't think we'd leave them by themselves, did you?"

We drove for a little while, and then Jonathan pulled up at a really nice looking hotel. He went in to register. I turned back to Mya and Shadow and said, "He sure surprised us, didn't he?"

They were both tilting their heads as if to say they understand me. He got back in the truck. "All set"

We walked into this huge room with a log canopy bed and a heart shaped Jacuzzi tub. On the floor was a big comforter.

"What's that for?" I asked.

"That's for Mya and Shadow to sleep on."

"How did it get here?"

"I requested it when I made the reservation. You didn't think I'd forget about them, did you?"

"Never," I said as I kissed him. He thought of everything.

He went over to the Jacuzzi tub, and then walked over to the dresser where a vase of roses sat. "These are for you, by the way," he said.

I couldn't believe this guy. He took one red, one purple and one yellow rose from the vase and walked over to the tub. He dropped the petals from the red rose in, then the yellow one and at last the purple one.

"Your bath awaits you my beautiful bride… my beautiful wife."

I walked over to him and gave him a kiss. "Thank you my handsome groom, my handsome husband. This tub looks awfully big for one person. It would be a waste of water," I laughed.

"Why, what are you suggesting my wife?" Jonathan laughed.

Before you knew it we were splashing around in the tub. Mya and Shadow were even joining in the fun. They were trying to put their paws in the water and running around the tub. Then, as we were laying back and letting the jets swirl the water around us, Jonathan asked, "How do you like that bed?"

TINA VELAZQUEZ

"I think it's beautiful."

"I'm going to make us one for the house when we get home," he said. "It'll be your wedding gift."

"You already gave me a wedding gift! The kitchen you're renovating."

"Oh we'll just say that was for helping me move in."

"I'm not going to argue this one because I really like the bed. But only on one condition…"

"What's that?" he smiled.

"That you let me help you. That way we both did it."

"No problem. In fact, I'd enjoy it. And it's funny you even said that, because I was going to ask you if ever I needed help on the weekends at work, if you'd come help me. I enjoyed you helping me so much at Alice's. I promise I won't work you hard," he laughed.

"Of course. You don't even need to ask. I would love too."

After that we retired to bed. That night was the most wonderful night of my life. Jonathan made sweet, gentle love to me until the wee hours of morning. He was the most loving person I had ever met. I was so lucky to have met him when I did. I couldn't imagine how my life would have turned out had I have not met him at Alice's. We fell asleep in each other's arms, talking about the life we were going to have together.

Chapter 29

The next morning, we woke up to the sun shining through the windows.

"Good morning my wife," Jonathan said.

"Good morning my husband," I smiled as I stretched.

"Ok time to get up and get going," he said.

"Where to?" I asked as Mya and Shadow jumped around wagging their tails.

"Well, The Smoky Mountains are about ten miles down the road. I had the front desk pack us a morning breakfast and we're going to take Mya and Shadow on a hike. They'll love it."

"Oh Jonathan, you think of everything," I said. I still couldn't believe my lucky fortune. We all piled in the truck and Jonathan stopped at the front desk. When he came back he was carrying a huge basket.

"Do you think you had them pack enough?"

"Well I hope so," he replied, laughing.

We went on a beautiful hike up to a waterfall. When we got to the top we spread out our picnic breakfast. The coffee was nice and hot. He even had them put dog treats and water in for the pups! He sure thought of everything. We spent the whole day out there with beautiful weather and the sun bright and shining. When we finally got back to the hotel, Jonathan turned to me and said, "Well how did you like your first day as my wife?"

TINA VELAZQUEZ

"I loved it," I replied.

"Well get used to it, because there's many more days like it coming," he said. He kissed me tenderly and hugged me until I almost couldn't breath! We both started laughing. "I'm sorry I just can't get enough of you," he laughed. "You are like a dream come true. I never would have believed I could be this happy."

Epilogue

The first year of marriage went by so fast! The two of us are extremely happy together and we finally made the house feel like home. We recently added a little cradle to our home. A week after our anniversary, we welcomed our new baby girl, Destiny, who came as quite the surprise! I'm still working for Alice, and just bringing another little one over with me everyday! She's been thrilled! Mya and Shadow watch over little Destiny as if she were their pup. Jonathan and I work together on the weekends while Jan watches Destiny. She was thrilled to be Godmother! And as for grandmothers, well, Destiny sure doesn't lack in that department! She had quite a few, in fact: Alice, June, Helen, Mary, Martha, Millie and Jill. As for The Senior Club, it's still going strong. In fact, we've gotten some new members, which also means Jan's gotten some new clients. We've all become one happy family. All my dreams have finally come true.